THE PINK PATH
Men Turning into Women the Fun Way!

Dracula Feminized Me
The Urban Hucow Farm
I Made Him Love Our Female Led Relationship
The Feminization of Jack
They Made Him a Sissy

Grace Mansfield

Copyright © 2021

ISBN: 9798760824080

I CHANGED MY HUSBAND INTO A WOMAN!

A delightful novel of total power exchange!

GRACE MANSFIELD

I Changed My Husband into a Woman!
Check it out at…
https://gropperpress.wordpress.com

TABLE OF CONTENTS

GRACE MANSFIELD

Dracula Feminized Me

An erotic horror short story!

PART ONE

We were in an inn. The biggest inn in Femsgaden, and there was nobody around us. And yet he looked like he thought somebody was going to jump out of the woodwork and snatch him.

He leaned forward and whispered. "People aren't just disappearing...they are changed."

Changed, huh. This was one weird job.

"Changed how?"

He was a rotund fellow with thick mustaches. He was wearing alpine clothing, and he looked stared at me as if asking if he could trust me. He was also the mayor of this little hamlet.

"They are changed...sexually."

I blinked. I had traveled a couple of hundred miles just to meet with a kook.

I sat back and smiled.

"No, please. I cannot go to the police. And we need help.

"And why can't you go to the police?" I was treating this like a joke, yet his look was frightened.

"Die Polizei are not...strong in this small district."

Femsgaden was small, and I could understand that. Femsgaden was considered the 'northern Berchtesgaden,' it was cold and icy, not much for tourists. There was probably one cop, and he was lazy.

"And the Bundespolizei?" The Bundespolizei were the federal police.

"The Bundespolizei...let us say they are...compromised."

I blinked.

"You're saying the federal police know who is kidnapping your people and...don't care? Won't do anything about it.

He looked down and nodded, and. I suddenly realized he was not just frightened, he was embarrassed. Embarrassed to be reporting kidnap victims? WTF?

I decided to string him along a bit and see where this joke went. I took the smile off my face and asked, "So tell me about this...how people are changed sexually."

He nodded, and gulped. He was doing a marvelous job of acting. I almost believed him, but...sexually changed? Come on.

He placed a folder on the table and opened it. "See?"

I stared at a picture of a man. Handsome fellow, curly brown hair, laughing eyes, skis over his shoulder. He looked like a player, in a Germanic sort of way.

On the opposite page was another picture. A woman. It was obvious that it was his sister.

"This..." I motioned towards the picture, "is..." I stopped and took note of the writing.

Same name, but feminized. Same birthdate. Same...everything. I looked at the faces more closely. I looked up at the mayor. "So you have twins."

He turned the page.

A blonde man, one raised eyebrow. Happy, looked like he might have been snapped while drinking. German beer was pretty strong stuff.

But on the opposite page was another picture. Another woman who looked....the same as him. Same features, same hair, but longer. Same birthdate. Another twin.

I was getting confused. "I don't see..."

He turned the page.

Another man and woman. Duplicates in every way, except one was male and one was female.

And another page, and another.

The folder had over twenty twins.

"So you have a lot of twins." I suddenly wondered if this was an elaborate practical joke. Except I didn't know anybody who would go this elaborate.

"Same people. He..." the mayor pointed at one of the men, "disappeared on a Friday." He pointed at the woman opposite. "She appeared on a Monday. Same for him and her," he flipped a page. "And him and her." He flipped a page. "Him and her," he flipped through the pages saying 'him and her' over and over.

"Wait a minute," I muttered, staring at the photographs. "You're telling me that these people disappear on Friday, get a sex change, and reappear on Monday?"

He nodded. His eyes were big and round.

Frightened.

"Have you tried talking to these people? Finding out what happened? I mean, people don't change sex over a weekend. It takes months and months, years, for a person to transition."

"I have tried, but...I am not like you. I am not an investigative reporter. I don't know what questions to ask, how to...follow up on their answers.

I sat back. This was just weird enough that I was actually interested. I couldn't believe it. "So what do you want me to do?"

"Find out what is happening. The young men of Femsgaden are disappearing. Who is changing them. How. Why."

I pondered while I held his gaze.

A secret sex change laboratory high in the mountains. Men changed into women against their will. Damned if it didn't sound like something I could sell. Even if only to the National Enquirer. that's right, the Germans have their own edition of that fabulous tabloid, and they paid well.

Of course it wouldn't be like real journalism. But 'real' journalism had taken it on the chin when Donald Trump had come into office. The whole American media had become a world laughing stock, so…the National Enquirer. Hmmm.

"So you want me to get the goods on these disappearing…these 'changing'…people. And, what? I write an expose? Tell the world about a bunch of perverts in your village?

He blinked. I had shocked him, but I had to. He had to understand where I was going with this. After all, I was going to get paid by him, he was actually hiring me to do a story which I would then sell to others. I didn't want there to be any misunderstanding.

He finally nodded.

I nodded. "Okay. I'll look into it."

"When?"

"Give me that folder. I'll study it, and I'll start investigating tonight."

Femsgaden, as I stated earlier was considered the northern Berchtesgaden. This was not necessarily a good thing, but it did pull in tourists.

Berchtesgaden, in the south of Germany was where Hitler vacationed. He had his famous 'Eagle's Nest' there, and his German Shepherd, Blondi, and his screening room where he watched his enemies be hung with piano wire.

But Berchtesgaden was now a sunny tourist resort. There was even a restaurant at the Eagle's Nest, the Berg-Restaurant Kehlsteinhaus.

Femsgaden, the northern Berchtesgaden was not so sunny. It was located almost in the Baltic Sea. It was fantastic for skiing, if you could get past the gloom.

And the lesser known fact, oddly downplayed by the German tourist industry, was that Hitler had spent much time there during the war. MUCH time. And he was't known for his skiing.

So why did Hitler spend so much time in this northern clime? And why didn't he bring his mistress, Eva Braun, with him? Or his dog?

He brought his cronies, Himmler and Goering, and a host of lesser known stars of the third reich. People like Eichmann, and Gosdek and Wahler, and…why?

I took the folder back to my hostel and studied it. I committed the names and faces of the women to memory. Wouldn't do much good to remember the men, they were…transformed.

The women were quite beautiful. Very beautiful.

As men they had been handsome fellows, but as women they were striking. A few shots showed me their bodies, and they were, to a woman, stacked and sexy.

And I'm not a guy who swings that way, if they really were guys, if you get my drift, but I couldn't deny their sex appeal.

That evening I went out on the town. I wasn't looking to make any contact, I just wanted to do a little recon on the landscape.

Femsgaden was an Alpine village that wasn't in the Alpines. The Alpines are a mountain range that runs through Europe, and the southern part of Germany. But this was a small northern mountain range, right off the Baltic. Still, the white washed buildings with criss crossed woodwork were there. The chimneys were tall and working overtime. The chill in these high parts was quite biting.

The town was accessible by a long winding drive through the ascending mountains, and it consisted of only a few streets, sandwiched in between the peaks.

The businesses in town were typical. Small shops that looked like they had been there for hundreds of years. A couple of modern ski shops. A handful of 'bierhalles.' Germans love their beerhalls.

So I walked up and down the main drag, and finally, to get a little warmth back in my bones, sauntered into a beerhall. I chose a seat near the large fireplace, ordered a liter of 'Bier,' and put my feet up.

It was nice in here, if a bit gloomy. The woodwork was old, but polished. The two waitresses were dressed in the traditional serving maid garb, puffy blouses and suspender dresses. And they were pretty well endowed, which made me smile.

I sate there and considered the elements of my story. Young men lured, or conked on the head, and…what? Taken to a laboratory and… experimented on? Given super chemicals that would instantly transform them from testosterone beasts to estrogen lassies?

Sitting there, feet up and sipping a beer, feeling the warmth and the bier seep into my bloodstream, it seemed laughable. Yet I knew the National Enquirer would buy it. It was just loony enough that—

The woman sat down two chairs from me. Her face was that unlined perfection, an ice queen. Her eyes were blue diamonds. Her red lips… they quirked. There was a joke somewhere in her buxom soul.

And I do mean buxom. She had curves on top of curves. She was a mountain range to herself.

She slipped off her ski jacket and gave me a better look. And thank God I have insurance in the event that my eyeballs fall out of my head. I mean, she was *that* good looking.

And she was one of the women in my folder.

Hiedi Braun. Once Heinrick Braun. From six foot to five foot six. From 180 pounds to 130 pounds. From short, crew cut to shoulder length waves. From a flat but muscular chest to...zowie.

She glanced at me, and I noted her eyes were scintillating blue. But her smile, it was...not happy.

I lifted my mug, "Buy you a drink?"

"Absolut," she murmured. Her voice was deep for a woman, but higher than a man's.

I waved a hand and her drink was delivered. She sipped, smiled wanly at me, "Danke schön."

I raised a hand in acknowledgement.

We were a couple of chairs apart, but we were alone, and in the warmth of the bierhalle there was an instant intimacy.

We sipped slowly, enjoyed the fire, and she asked, "Tourist?" She spoke English with a slight accent.

"Journalist," I answered. "But I'm on vacation. But I'm thinking about doing a piece on Femsgaden."

She nodded. Didn't say much, then suddenly stood up and came to the chair next to me.

"Journalist. Sounds fascinating. Do you travel the world?"

A little, not much."

"What do you write about? All the big news stories of the day?"

"More like all the small stories. Every once in awhile, if I'm in the right place, I get picked up, assigned, but that's not the glamour one would think. There's actually more glamour to sitting in a bierhalle with a lovely maiden." I raised my glass to her.

She smiled, actually seemed to overcome her melancholy for a moment, and raised her own mug.

"So you do not go into war zones. Or meet presidents."

I laughed. "No war zones, thank you. But every once in a while I'll meet a president. They're boring fellows."

And we chatted, light, trading snippets about our lives.

"I am editor for children's books. I was."

"Was?" I asked.

"Still am, but..." she shrugged, and there was an infinity of sadness in that little motion.

"Time to pick up and move on, eh?"

"Something like that."

A couple entered the bierhalle. Laughing, joking, ordered some bier and headed for a booth in a corner.

We watched them, and she smiled. "He is cheating on his wife."

"Hunh." I examined their dress, their manner. "How do you know they aren't man and wife? Or betrothed."

Hiedi chuckled. A manly chuckle in a female body. "He moves like he doesn't want to be seen. She is too happy. They are cheaters."

Another person entered the hall, but I took no notice of him.

Hiedi said, "I know because I—." she stopped, redirected her obvious senrence. "I would do that if I were a man."

"You'd cheat, eh? You know what I have to ask now?"

She turned back to me with a lift of the eyebrows. "Yes?"

"Are you a loose woman?"

She laughed, then sobered. Then she cried. Right in the middle of the damn bierhalle.

A man slid into the seat next to her. The fellow who had entered and who I had ignored.

But I notice everybody. It is my job. See who is who, describe who is who. Why hadn't I noticed him?

He wore black, and a black cloak. It was light garb for a cold clime, but…

"Heidi, my dear," he soothed. "You must not scare the young man."

"I'm sorry," instantly the tears stopped. Stopped as if he had slapped her in the face and shocked her to stop.

He placed a hand on her shoulder and smiled. A small smile. Just enough of a smile to reveal bright, white teeth, and I began to really study him.

He was slender, about my height, which is five eight. His complexion was pale, as if he never saw the sun. His hair was full and rich and slicked back. Shiny.

But it was his eyes that were the most striking.

Almost no whites to them. Almost all pupil. And no blinking. Eventually the no blinking would unnerve me. I mean, who doesn't blink? You have to blink to water the eyes! But he didn't blink. He just stared and those big pupils dissected, devoured, examined.

"Now clean yourself up and come back."

"Yes, Count Dacian." She sprang from the chair like a frightened animal and headed for the restroom.

Count Dacian watched her for a moment, his eyes lidded and his smile a simple line revealing little. He turned to me.

"You must forgive Hiedi."

"Nothing to forgive."

I was fascinated by this slender wisp. He was languid, yet he emitted sparks. He was lazy, yet I could feel energy manifesting, coming out of him in waves. His was a vitality that underwhelmed, and ate out your supports, but…in spite of that energy there was that about him that would go unnoticed. Like when he had entered the bierhalle and slid right past my trained eye.

I wondered at this quality. This hidden shade of personality dwelling within. At how he had moved in and controlled Hiedi.

He raised an arm and the waitress placed a bier in front of me almost instantly.

"You are a tourist?"

I smiled.

"Yes? What is funny?"

His accent was funny. It was thick and overblown, like he wasn't used to talking to people.

"We were just talking about that," I waved my mug in the direction of the gone Hiedi.

"Ah," he smiled.

"And you live around here?"

"I don't look like a tourist?" That wan smile again. A bit of Mona Lisa in the man.

"You look...comfortable."

He raised his eyebrows and nodded most pleasantly. "I live in the castle on the hill."

"Oh?" I tilted my head.

"You didn't know there was a castle?"

"I didn't."

"I...inherited it. It is a quite wonderful place. I am dedicated to returning it to its original form."

"Is that difficult?" I was actually curious. "I mean, do you rebuild structures using original tools form the era? That sort of thing?"

"A bit, but not much actual physical adjustment is needed. It is mostly a process of introducing..." he thought, then smiled, "Ambient. What you would call ambience."

Hiedi returned at that moment, and even though she was the point of my story, I was sorry. There was just something very magnetic about Count Dacian. He wasn't likable, exactly, but he...compelled. No, not compelled, I don't know the exact word, but he drew one in, made you want to learn more about him.

"I'm sorry, Count Dacian," she murmured. Her lipstick was fresh, her mascara repaired. She was subdued.

"My dear, not to worry. I know how difficult it is. You just go on and have a good time."

He had stood up and she was looking up at him, gazing into those black pools. Searching his eyes as if looking for stars on a cloudy night.

And worried.

But what did she have to worry about?

Count Dacian turned to me. "I must go."

"Before you go," I hesitated, "Do you...would it be possible to see your castle some day?"

Hiedi drew in her breath.

Dacian smiled. "Anything is possible."

Then he was gone, and he was gone like a swoosh, like a turn of his cape and he...disappeared.

I sat and meditated over this mysterious man. Owned a castle. A personality that seemed like a fading. Dressed in black...like the bad guy in a bad movie.

"I am sorry I cried." Hiedi sat down next to me and placed a hand on my arm.

I turned my attention to the lovely and smiled. "I'm sorry I made you cry."

She blinked. "But you didn't..." Then she figured it out. She smiled. Not much of a smile, but something. "You joke with me."

"Some people say my jokes make people cry."

"You are a nice man." It was sudden. A blurt. And we stared at each other.

Then I cracked a grin, "About that I am sure you are wrong."

"No, no."

She reached for her mug and looked at it, then she looked at me. "Will you get drunk with me to night?"

I lifted an eyebrow.

"I am sorry. I am too forward. But I am sad. I need to...I need happiness."

I can't guarantee you happiness, but I can do a little drinking."

She smiled, and there was actual joy, or perhaps relief, in her beautiful mouth. She put her arms around my biceps, leaned close to me. "Let us find a booth, we can drink and get drunk. You can tell me of all the women you have been with. And I will envy you."

"Me being with women?" I laughed, assuming that she had just made a lingual faux pas.

"Oh, I mean," she was flustered, and she was embarrassed. The odd thing, and I would think on this later, is that she didn't blush. Or perhaps I didn't see her blush through her make up. Or, perhaps she was incapable of blushing. But she still had that look of somebody who was embarrassed.

We sat in a booth and ordered bier after bier. And it was German bier, strong enough to knock an elephant on its ass. And I was no elephant.

We talked, and reminisced, and she sat so close to me. Almost clung to me.

And it was wonderful.

And I had all these weird, snarky, odd, kinky, scared thoughts going through my head.

Had she really been a man? Had she changed from man to woman in three days? Friday a man and Monday a girl?

The thought of being with a man frightened me. I'm not a

homophobe...well, maybe I am, a little. I mean, when it came time to kiss and cuddle.

But what were we doing, Hiedi and I, if not kissing and cuddling? Without the kissing, but with the promise of it.

We drank our bier, and her breath was cool, a freshness on my face. Her hands were small and touched mine, touched my face.

Sometimes we were leaning towards each other, as if to kiss, but I held myself back. Inches from those beautiful lips *Was she a man?* Sometimes she squeezed my hand, soft motions to emphasize what we were talking about, and it felt like she was making sure I was a red-blooded boy.

We talked of her childhood, and she presented it as female, or at least didn't present it as male.

I told her a couple of college stories, those wild and uninhibited times, and she laughed at the pranks I had played, or had played on me.

The night grew long. People came and left. Couples, groups. Drinking pitchers, then sliding out the door, leaving my consciousness as if drifting into a fog, never to be seen again.

There was only her...*was she a man?*...and she was so beautiful. At one point she whispered in my ear and I shivered. Her cool breath, those red lips touching my flash.

Was she a man?

Then the night was upon us full.

Customers left and the population in that bierhalle dwindled.

I was drunk, but there was something in her personality that kept me sober.

The fear that she was a man.

Yet, when it came time to leave, I stood up with her, and we walked down the street together. Arms around each other, protecting each other against the cold and the vicious northern wind sweeping in off the Baltic.

We walked, and I realized we were walking towards my hostel.

"Where do you live?" I asked, my drunken eyes searching the landscape as if for her home.

"In the castle, but I would not go home just yet."

"The castle? Count Dacian's castle?"

"Yes. He is my...benefactor. He helps me. He takes care of me."

Her statement told me a lot, without telling me anything. He had come in to the bierhalle and rescued her from her excessive emotion, as if he had known she was going to cry. Then he had departed, as if he was puffed away by a breath, and left her to me. Left a defenseless woman with a horn dog.

Okay, maybe I'm not a horn dog.

Well, maybe I am.

Heck, what guy isn't a horn dog?

And he had just left her with me.

A stranger, somebody he didn't know.

Not that I looked like a serial killer or a rapist or anything, but…but what?

Why was I pondering such silliness and the motivations of some guy who wasn't even there when I had a beautiful woman in my grasp?

But was she a woman?

"I can take you to the castle?"

"No…no. I cannot go home. Not yet." she grinned, drunkenly, and said, "I turn into a pumpkin at dawn."

I laughed. "I think it's supposed to be midnight."

She sobered. "No. It is dawn."

She turned to me then, clutched me, hugged me, as if she was in fear of her very life.

Then she moved back slightly and tilted her head, looked up at me.

Those blue eyes, fire and ice.

Was she a man?

I moved my face closer to hers. Her red lips, her cool breath, I felt like I was in a spell.

Was she a man?

Like a dream our lips touched, meshed, and it was like a bomb went off in my head. I felt blasted, nervous, out of breath, and I wanted more.

She pushed me back. We were both breathing hard.

"Take me to your room."

I did. Without hesitation. And I didn't even wonder if she was a man. The way she kissed, the way she devoured my soul with her lips… there was no doubt that she was a woman.

We entered my lodgings, climbed the narrow stairs, stopped to kiss on the landing, then entered my room.

Standing with the curtains open, the moonlight blasting us, washing us in purity.

Laying on the bed, fully clothed, feeling each other. Kissing.

I took her blouse off and marveled with my lips. Her breasts were big, full, and heavy. The nipples were particularly delicious.

She stripped my pants off and went down on me. She made me moan and groan, and rubbed my knob until I was on the very edge.

Then we were completely naked, she was on her back, and I was between her legs, my cock brushing against her portal.

I tickled her labia and made her giggle. I bit her clitoris and made her twitch and hold on.

She held my balls and threatened to pop them with a squeeze.

"I could, you know. I am very strong. They would crumple like ping pong balls, then actually burst. Blood would come through my fingers and I would lick it.

She was serious, sober for all our drunkenness, and threatening me.

"Go ahead," I laughed, and I smothered her with kisses again.

She pulled me into her depths. My eyes widened. She was ice and fire on the inside. It was like she was rubbing my cock with ice cubes, but so fast that I burst into flames.

She held to me, smiled up at me, was happy for me.

"It is good, no?"

"Oh, yes. It is good," I gasped.

Then I began to squirt. It was like a massive hand just squeezed my whole body and my pecker was the relief valve. I squirted semen and again, and my whole body was shaking and shivering. I had never had a cum like this in m life.

I finished, and lay upon her.

She let me. Seemed to enjoy my weight upon her.

I rolled off. "You didn't cum," I stated. "Let me get you off."

She shook her head. "No. No. I don't cum much. Besides. It makes me happy to make you cum. Let me have that."

I watched her watching me. She was serious, and who was I to argue?

We kissed again. Not for lust, but just for the enjoyment of a kiss without the need. Then we talked, in whispers, as if we might wake somebody up.

And, somewhere in there, we slept.

At least I did.

I woke up when the sun came through the window and struck me in the eyes. I smiled. I had had such a wonderful time. And the idea that Hiedi was a man…sheer silliness, and I would tell the mayor that there was no story here. That he—I opened my eyes.

I had left the folder sticking out of a brief case. And a picture had been visible. Hiedi must have seen the picture, gotten curious, and opened the folder.

And looked at the picture.

Maybe she even recognized the girl in the photo.

But in looking through the photos she would certainly recognize herself.

And now the folder was open on top of my dresser. And it was open to…her picture.

Fuck.

I got up and looked at the folder. There was a note on top of her picture.

I read the note. It didn't upbraid me, or chastise me, or berate me in any manner.

Alexander, thank you, but you must go. I have to tell Count Dacian, but he will already know. He sees through my eyes. But I am writing this note without looking. You must go, and before the night. Tonight will be too late. but if you leave now…he won't follow.

That was it. No signature. And the lines and the writing was a bit sloppy, as if she had been writing with her eyes closed, forming her phrases and sentences by feel and knowingness.

I must leave today. Before Count Dacian came for me.

But why would Count Dacian wait for the night?

And so what if he came for me?

I was a reporter, I had done nothing wrong. Possessing the photos, and the short write ups on missing people, that was not a crime.

So what if he came for me?

And, as a matter of fact, I wanted him to come for me. I wanted to know what he had to do with Hiedi, who was supposed to have been a man until…she wasn't.

I blinked, remembering the night. No, Hiedi was a woman. Through and through. There was no doubt about that.

But Count Dacian was mixed up in this somehow, and I needed to have a little talk with the good Count.

I needed to have a big talk.

And I was sure that there was a story here.

Maybe it wasn't men being turned into women, but it was something.

Count Dacian had a secret. I didn't know if he was a simple Svengali, but he was…something.

And as long as I remained in public view there was nothing he could do to me. What was he going to do? Kidnap me right in the middle of town? Maybe in a bierhalle crowded with people?

I thought not.

And I looked forward to my meeting with the mysterious Count Dacian.

PART TWO

The day moved slowly. I had breakfast in a small cafe with a big view. I watched people trundle along mountain paths on the way to ski areas. I watched businesses open.

A cold wind came up and scoured the village.

I spent some time in my hostel in a small reading room. I examined the days news, and it was boring. I didn't care if there was a war and people were getting killed...I had my own war right here in Femsgaden.

I went for a long walk.

I sat in a shop and sipped hot chocolate. Heiße Schokolade they called it. It was more bitter than American hot chocolate, but, in a way, better. Germans don't allow GMO in their foods, and I guess this went all the way down to a simple cup of heiße schokolade.

I went to the library and researched the area.

Yes, Hitler and his friends, but there was a history even before that. There was violence here, but it was subdued. But the oddest thing was that while there was war in the world, and even in this area, it never really touched Femsgaden. Soldiers would come, get drunk, and depart.

I wondered what happened to the soldiers when they had too much to drink, got in fights. But there wasn't much on that, just a subtle peace with a sheen of violence that..disappeared.

Femsgaden. Hmmm. What is your secret?

The afternoon waned and, finally, night arrived.

I knew where the castle was, and I could have walked up a lonely mountain road, taken a turn through some gates that, in the newspaper photo I saw, were hanging loose at the hinges, and walked up aa twisty, curvy road that, again the newspapers, was supposedly built for horse and carriages.

And the carriages that were pictured were of the funeral variety.

Except that would have been twenty miles or more of walking.

And there were no Ubers or taxis in Femsgaden. The hamlet just wasn't that big.

So, I waited.

Hiedi had said Count Dacian would come for me. So all I had to do was wait.

I had more hot chocolate. No bier tonight. Tonight I would be working. Possibly confronting the lion in his den.

The sun went down at exactly five fourteen. By the almanac. Just slid into a mountain notch and...poof. Gone.

Exactly one minute later Count Dacian walked into the bierhelle.

He wore the same black suit, no protection against the cold. And the same black clock, a line of red trim on the inside, a swirl that was not much protection against the elements.

Yet there was that about him that was...elemental. He needed no protection against the elements because he *was* an element.

He didn't look around to find me, he knew where I was, and he walked on a straight line towards me. He was smiling, amused, like he was the Mona Lisa and had just stuck a match in somebody's sole.

The night previous he had slithered past people, unnoticed.

Tonight they saw him coming, were startled, and stepped aside.

He sat down next to me, flung his cloak out a bit to sit, and settled in like he had been carved there.

"Ah, herr reporter. Mister journalist." His smile was an unwavering, fixed point of insanity. His eyes glittered, like a flashlight way at the bottom of a mine.

"Alexander will do. Or Alex, if you prefer."

"Would you like a beer? Or other beverage?"

A moment of whimsy, I nodded.

He raised a hand and the waitress scuttled up. Last night she had not even seen Count Dacian. Tonight she seemed to be in fear of him.

"Coke High for my friend," Count Dacian.

I blinked. Bourbon and Coke. My drink of choice. How had he known?

"I have a talent for reading minds, my friend."

"Do tell?" I was diffident, unconcerned. Though I felt my heart fluttering somewhere in side my chest.

"For instance, you would like to know if I am just a Svengali."

I tilted my head slightly. He was good. But he had probably conversed with people like me before. There was a certain amount of predictability to me. What he said next shattered that notion.

"And you have a fascination for Herr Hitler."

Now that was reaching deep.

I stared at him, he smirked, and my drink arrived.

I sipped, and found that the sip turned into a gulp. Yeah. I was getting nervous. As a reporter my questions usually put people on the ropes, made them nervous. But I felt like the shoe was on the other foot now.

"Hiedi loves you, you know."

At my lack of response he continued, "But then she is new to her role. She thinks she is supposed to fall in love with a man she has fucked. It is a common failing of the young.

"What did you do to her?"

"Hiedi? I made her dreams come true. Of course dreams, as you

19

might suspect, are not usually what you expect."

"So what now?"

"That is up to you. You can go off and write your silly story. Stories have been written before, but the newspapers have a curious habit of not printing them."

"You've bought off the newspapers?"

"I know. It seems unlikely. Small town Svengali buys off international news media. But you should know…it's all fake news, anyway."

Fuck. this guy hit it on the head. But, still…

"Or you can come for a visit."

"To the castle? Your castle?"

"Absolut. My home. You may see the construction, or should I say 're-construction.' You may experience the ambient. You may, if you are lucky, even see what it is I do to the people you are so concerned about."

Man, this was too much. Talk about dreams come true. To visit a serial killer, or whatever, and observe his methods first hand. But…did I risk a serial killer? Or whatever he was?

He smiled, and did that mind reading thing again. He raised a hand and summoned the owner of the bierhalle.

Helmut Noether was short and chubby, sort of like the mayor, and he twisted his hands in his apron nervously.

"A pen and paper, Herr Noether."

A pen and paper were brought to us. Quickly. Count Dacian began scribbling. He handed me a sheet of paper.

For scribbling, his penmanship was majestic and flowing, and his words were easy to read.

I, Count Dacian, am taking the journalist Alexander Sutwell, to visit my castle. He is in good health, and if he is not in good health come Monday morning, it is my responsibility.
Count Dacian

It was dated.

He took the paper from my hand and handed it to Herr Noether. "Mr. Sutwell will be by on Monday to pick this up. Please hold it until then. If Mr. Sutwell doesn't show up you will take this to the police on Tuesday morning. Am I clear?

"Precisely," and Noether clicked his heels like he was a Nazi clicking jackboots together.

"And you will take this, too." He turned to me, "Your cell phone, please?"

I didn't like being separated from my cell phone.

He raise a finger and said, "Ah…of course." He reached into his own pocket and pulled out a cell phone. He handed it to Noether and smiled.

Noether actually didn't want to take the phone. He was visibly sweating. But he did take it, he snapped a picture of myself and Count Dacian sitting together, like old friends, though my face was a bit shiny with perspiration and my mouth was curved in worry.

He handed the phone to Noether. "And this will go to the police also," he smiled at me. "Unless Alex picks it up on Monday."

And it was done. There was no reason for me not to visit the Count in his castle.

On one hand, I was scared. I don't know why. Except that if the good Count did do something to me then the evidence of my passing would do me no good, no matter how many police looked at it.

And, on the other hand, I wanted to go. I needed to get to the heart of this story. I needed to find out what had happened to the men who... who changed.

Count Dacian stood up, his cloak settled about him. "Herr Noether, as always, you please me with you wonderful hospitality."

Noether nodded, muttered some nicety, and backed away. Holding the sheet of paper and the cell phone.

"Shall we go?" said Count Dacian to me.

We exited the bierhalle and a coach was waiting.

I don't mean a coach, like as in a bus, but as in a horses drawn carriage.

Black with black trim. An exercise in night. Even the horses were black. A dim figure was huddled atop the carriage, ready to drive, but not showing me his visage.

Yet he held a whip, and that one thing...it poured a dram of fear into my chest. Something about being taken somewhere by a nondescript person...it shivered me.

But Count Dacian opened the door and I stepped up and into the coach.

On the street nobody was looking, nobody was staring. As if, like the Count on that first night, the coach was a slippery thing that avoided perceptions.

I sat back in a comfortable leather seat. Yet it didn't smell like leather. It smelled...old. Well used. Polished.

The Count closed the door and sank into the seat across from me. The carriage immediately jolted into motion.

We rode through the town, and the drapes were drawn. Count Dacian, with the ever present smile, inspected me.

Finally, we had left the bounce of the cobblestones, he said, "You have questions?"

Oh, baby, did I have questions. I started off with an easy one. "Do you change men into women?"

His eyes arched and there was a delighted feel to him. "I do. And sometimes I change women into men, but not very often. It is mostly men who are the...more curious."

I had the feeling he was going to say 'perverts,' but I accepted his word without comment.

"May I record our conversation?"

"Absolut."

I took out my recorder and held it on my lap. "For the record then, do you change men into women?"

He repeated his answer happily.

"And why do you do this?"

"Well, technically, while I am the instrument of change, the desire must come from them. They must want to be changed."

Huh. That was a whole line of inquiry in itself. I kept myself to the point. "And how do you do this?"

I release the soul, and the soul makes the decision. Of course it takes a lot of guidance, there is much fear, and a bit of pain." He smiled. "Actually, a lot of pain, but people will go through what they go through to realize their dreams."

The carriage was lurching a bit, and we were shifted to one side, then the other. We had turned off the road already, gone through the gates, and were heading up a narrow road. I was glad the curtains were drawn, for the edge of the road dropped off to a sheer drop along the way.

"Did you know of the castle's history when you bought it?"

"History? Oh, of course, you are talking about Herr Hitler." He spoke as if Adolf was still alive.

"Herr Hitler wished to change, but, alas, he was one of my few failures. You are aware that he was born with one testicle. Something was left out of the dear boy, and for that reason I couldn't help him." He shook his head sadly. Then he brightened up.

"I was, however, able to help him, to give him advice, in other matters. Him and his merry band of men."

"You mean Himmler and Goering and..." I cast about in my head for other names and came up with, "...and Eichmann and Mengele."

Count Dacian sat back and sighed. "Ah, yes. Eichmann. And Josef. My dear friends." He leaned forward. "You realize they were, in their own pitiful ways, trying to emulate what I do?"

I waited. He sat back again.

"Herr Eichmann could only transform partially. Again, something was left out of him, rendering my methods less than successful." He shook his head slowly and made a tsking sound. "But Mengele, now he was changeable, and he was a genius. In his own way, of course."

There was something about the Count that was actually making me dizzy, as if I was being taken through his memories, but without knowing what I was seeing, or perhaps experiencing things that...that...

"Josef, with his torments and tortures. He played with transforming people. All his methods were aimed towards that eventuality. He had seen what I could do, he had experienced what I could do, and he thought he could duplicate what I do with his injections and experiments. He would cause great pain, play with twins, try to assess reactions, all to the point of doing what I could already easily do."

Oh, man. I hoped my recorder was getting all this. No crime here, but a delusion of grandeur that was, even to a jaded reporter as myself, incredible.

I asked him questions then, and he was quick and easy in his answers. Seemed proud of his sadism. Of his perverse character.

Finally, the carriage drew to a halt.

"We are here." The Count announced happily. He opened the door and we dismounted from the coach.

It was dark and my eyes slowly adjusted.

It was dark because we were in a valley, and the valley was of sheer cliffs. The moon, a small, pale orb, offered no warmth, but a little light.

I squinted, tried to relax and let my eyes do their work.

The castle was set into the back of the valley. It was medium size on the outside, six stories with two turrets that reached up another four stories.

It was made of carved, black stone. A marvelous jigsaw puzzle, inset with windows, crowned with battlements. There were chimneys, but it was obvious there were no fires in the hearths below.

I could easily see an army bashing its head against these stout and fiercesome walls. Spears and large stones would rain down, buckets of burning oil poured over helmeted heads. It was as if I could actually hear the screams, feel the pain as—

"Please don't step back." Count Dacian's hand gripped my biceps. His hand was slender, but his grip was like an armwrestler's.

I looked behind me, I had been backing up, a response to the screams in my imagination, and I was on the edge of a precipice. One more step and I would have tumbled over, fallen a thousand feet to impale myself on shards of stone.

I stepped forward, and he let go. In the darkness I stared at him.

I had the feeling he would have enjoyed watching me tumble from the heights, the way my skin would have been flayed by sliding down the sharp edges, the way my bones would have broken. How I would have lain, a bag of broken bones not easily retrieved.

"Thank you."

He just smiled.

Because he had worse things in store for me than a tumble over a cliff?

He led me across the courtyard. The paving stones were well fit, smooth from traffic over the centuries.

The door was a huge arch, two doors, and they swung back without help from human hand. Big, monstrous doors of oak, kept together by bands of iron. A keyhole for a monster key, but I had a feeling these doors, as they had opened without human hand, would lock without human help.

The inside of the castle open up to a huge great room. The ceilings were forty feet high, crisscrossed with tree trunks stripped of bark. Above the beams, the ceiling proper, was stone, and it was the most marvelous masonry I had ever seen. I could tell the shape of the blocks by the different grain, but they were fitted together without gap. They created a dome which supported itself, a thousand tons of carved boulder.

The walls were built of rough blocks of stone. Again, there were no gaps in the seams, but it was easier to see the way they had been piled upon each other.

Ensconced in walls were iron torch holders, no electric lights here. The torches gave off a flickering glow that was bright enough to read, as long as the print was large.

High chandeliers hung about the room, further adding to the illumination. There were hangings on the walls, battle scenes, wolf hounds and hunts. Nothing remotely Christian in attitude.

And a lone picture at the end of the room, above the largest fireplace I had ever seen. There was no fire lit, however. The picture was of Count Dacian.

He followed the path of my eyes and noted the picture. "I am arrogant, I know. But all truly great men are, must have arrogance underpinning their character. You don't need to believe me, if you wish."

Oh, Lord. There were so many things I didn't want to believe here. This whole place smelled of...of...

"I know, words fail you."

"Where is the construction you spoke of?"

"There are places, mostly on the outer walls, where daylight fights the night, where we have scaffolding and the laborers come from the village. But they are not visible during the night, unless you wish to walk along the edge of cliffs."

He grinned.

"I'll take your word for it. Is...is Hiedi here?"

"Most assuredly. We will come upon her shortly. But first, let me give you a tour."

We walked through the downstairs, he showed me the kitchens, the servants quarters—though there were no servants, to speak of—small rooms dedicated to weaving, to storage, to other purposes known only to people of a thousand years previous.

I was allowed full use of my cell phone and I snapped hundreds of pictures.

Up a wind of stairs and through the higher floors. Sometimes bed chambers, sometimes sitting rooms.

Up into one of the turrets. It was a round room and he opened a double door and we stepped onto a high balcony. I could see the lights of Femsgaden twinkling through wisps of clouds. Though the moon was unchanged in size, it felt like we were closer. But certainly no warmer.

Then down the stairs, through quarters, and to the ground floor.

"Most impressive, Count," I murmured. "But I have seen no staff." *Nor hint of Hiedi...or of any of the others you have kidnapped.*

"Ah, yes. The best for last. Come."

He led me back to the kitchen, then down a circle of stairs, far down the steps. The air, surprisingly, was not cold. It was more like the absence of cold. But the absence of heat, also.

Down, down.

We came to the dungeons. Arches of crumbling stone, iron bars. And...instruments. I saw a rack. Fortunately, it was dusty.

Other equipment, however, was not.

There was a Judas Cradle, which was just a pyramid upon which helpless victims were lowered, the point to enter their lower cavity, their own weight to impale themselves slowly.

A couple of iron maidens, with sharpened spikes that glinted... except for the points, which looked to be rusted. I touched a spike and a gritty substance came off on my finger. Dried blood.

A Spanish donkey, which was a length of wood with an edge for people to sit on, and be split.

And there were chairs with spikes on the seats, collars with spikes in them, pears of anguish, to be opened inside body cavities, and so much more.

And while there were spiderwebs abounding, on some of the instruments there was no spider web, yet small hints of dried blood.

We came to the end of the room, and a final door.

"What's behind here?" I asked.

"Your dreams," he said without expression, merely watching me.

I waited. When it was obvious he wasn't going to say anything, I was forced to ask, "How do you know my dreams."

"The same way I can read your mind."

I waited. And, finally, "Can I go in?"

"If you wish."

I held his gaze for a moment, watched those dark pools watch me. I reached for the door latch. He said nothing. I opened it.

Down the stairs, he followed me. silently. I made foot noises, he didn't. He glided, a cloud across the ground.

Down and down, much deeper than the trip to the dungeons. I had a feeling we were angling right into the heart of the mountains.

The walls began dripping.

There were seams, it was one rock, one giant stone, that we were walking through.

And I heard voices. I glanced at Count Dacian, but he said nothing. His lips were slightly pursed, he merely regarded me. No emotion. Just… watching.

We came out in another dungeon. The individual cells were not fronted by iron bars, but by an ancient criss cross of flat iron. Like a latticework.

We walked past the cells, and I could hear moans, some sexual, some tortured, but when I looked into the cells there was nobody there.

The end of the dungeon was not lit. It was dark, a shadow, and from out of the shadow came Hiedi.

"Alex?" she squealed happily and ran towards me. She was wearing a peignoir, open in front, her breasts, so large, bounced. Her arms were out, and she embraced me.

"Oh, Alex! I am so sorry!" She smothered my face with kisses.

"For what?"

"I shouldn't have scared you with that stupid note. That was bad of me, and I'm so sorry."

"Don't be. It brought me here, didn't it?"

I smiled her. She had her hands on my face and she pulled me to her, touched my lips with hers. I could feel her, so cool, yet her touch was so hot.

"Come, I want you to meet my friends."

I looked behind me as she led me towards the darkness, but the Count was no longer there.

Yet I had the feeling he was watching.

Once in it, the darkness was not so dark. It was gloomy, but it was like I could see everything even better. As if blue was a brilliant light, and I could see in blue.

"This is Gunter," a slender fellow floated out of the darkness. He smiled and embraced me. There was no threat, he was just welcoming me.

"He used to be Grendel. And this is Ursula, she used to be Jurgen. And this is…"

People crowded around me, embraced me, gave me their love. I found I was almost floating with the crowd, they had surrounded me so closely.

Finally, far back in the blue darkness, I managed to ask, "Hiedi, you introduce me, then you say the men were women, and the women were men."

"Of course, silly, because they were."

And I knew she spoke the truth, for I had seen several of the men turned to women in my pictures.

"But how is that possible?"

Hiedi smiled. "We can show you, but we can't tell you."

"Make me into a woman?"

"Of course."

"I don't think I—"

"Not forever, you silly. Just for the weekend. You can change back whenever you want. Wouldn't you like to be a woman?"

In my mind: *I had never wanted to. I loved women, but...to be one?*

Yet: *to walk in a different body. To wear different clothes. And... make up.*

And I: *wondered, and tossed about the idea that I was an investigative reporter. This was what I had come to find out.*

I cogitated: *Besides, it can't be done. They'll give me some drug and I'll think I've changed. It's all mass hallucination. None of this is really real.*

Thinking: *I can feel Count Dacian. He's here somewhere, watching, laughing. And I can prove him wrong.*

My heart light, not admitting to the ambience, the feel, the pervasive spirit that haunted this cursed castle, I said. "Okay."

I was in a party. Everybody jumping and clapping their hands, celebrating my decision.

"Come along, then."

They escorted me, those beautiful and bountiful people. They walked me further into the gloom, and we came to the room at the end of the gloom.

And I walked as if in a dream, rejoicing in their cheer and sincere welcome.

We walked further into the room at the end of the gloom. Deeper into the dream. The world, the real world, became a memory, and we floated through a fog of wonderful, good humor.

Came to a bed.

And stopped.

Hiedi said to me, "I found you, I should be allowed to sleep with you through the change."

There were nods.

"Okay," I said.

"Then take off your clothes and lay down. We will welcome you properly."

I did so, and lay on the bed. Naked. My penis hard. I had cum the night before, but I was surrounded by luscious bodies, eager bodies. And I felt my lust abounding.

"Here then, take the potion."

I was handed a bottle. I looked at it, I smelled it, then I shrugged and quaffed the thing.

Hiedi took the bottle and handed it to somebody else.

"First is Gretchen."

Gretchen was a luscious peach with red hair and a large rack. She came out of the crowd, was handed up to the bed by a few men, and she strode across the mattress to me. She straddled me, and she sank down.

I was impaled, quickly and easily. Or, rather, I impaled her.

She groaned and grabbed her tits and clawed them.

She ground her hips down and corkscrewed upon me. I felt my cock swelling, getting ready to spit, but I couldn't, and Gretchen began to cum.

She wailed, slapped her pussy, and exhausted herself on me.

They lifted her off me.

"This is Ingrid." Another woman, this one blonde with heavy hips and a smile that wouldn't quit, was handed up, and squatted over me.

She surrounded my cock, began to palpate my shaft with her pussy. She was cool, like ice, but she made me hot, like lava.

She came, a caterwauling scream of desperation, then collapsed on me.

She was lifted off and another woman was put upon me. "This is Monica."

"This is Gisela."

"This is Suzanne."

They came and they came, but, woman after woman, I couldn't.

"I can't cum!" I screamed at one point, my dick wrung out and my balls aching.

"Why would you want to?" Hiedi whispered in my ear. "You cum and it's over. You stay hard and we get to welcome you.

"Petra."

"Suzanne."

I was hurting, yelling, but then even my yells subsided. There was nothing I could do but suffer.

Time is different down there, below the earth, where demons and devils live. Friday night should have turned to Saturday, to Sunday, but it didn't. It just stayed Friday, and women took me, used me, discarded me.

"Let me go!" I cried.

""Not once it has started," whispered Hiedi. "Afterwards, you may undergo this again and change back."

My body began to transform. The continual fucking, I grew breasts. Large breasts. I could feel them, and then I could feel my dick shrinking.

Women took longer to cum on me, and they complained.

There came a time when my dick was no longer a dick. It was a slit, and the men lined up.

Now I screamed at a pitch I had never dreamed of.

I'm not a homophobe, except when I was.

The men embraced me, kissed me, and I reached new levels of insanity.

They penetrated me, and I felt what a woman feels.

And I knew that the changes were still happening inside.

Balls were turning to ovaries. My nervous system was being transformed. My bones were being shaped, my fat was being redistributed.

I felt different.

And still they fucked me.

"This is Hans."

"This is Walter."

"This is…"

Until consciousness dwindled. Until insanity could no longer sustain me. Until there was nothing left but to give up.

I awoke. I was in a bed. It was daytime.

I was a woman.

I got out of bed. It was cold out, I had no clothes, but I didn't feel the cold. I felt like I would never feel cold again, nor even heat, as long as I lived.

There was a peignoir hanging on the back of the door. That was all, and I put it on. Not to warm, for I didn't need that. Not for modesty, but for convention.

And it was sort of sexy.

I left the room, walked down the hall bare footed. The cold stones didn't hurt me.

Down the stairs.

Hiedi was in the great room, sitting in a large chair. She stood up when I came to her.

She hugged me. She was cool, and I didn't feel her heart beating.

But it had to be beating. How could she live without a heart? I phrased my thought.

"How can you live without a heart?"

She smiled and held my hands, two women facing each other in sexy peignoirs.

"I don't need a heart to love. I just need a body to caress." She caressed me.

And I had to respond. I caressed her.

"How do you feel?" she asked.

"Horny," I answered honestly.

"Yes. Isn't it wonderful? And terrible all at the same time?"

"But I need to cum!"

"Of course you do. And you will. Just as soon as you bring someone to us."

"Some one to—"

"Yes, that is how we grow. Find somebody who has the inner dream, a man wanting to be a woman, a woman wanting to be a man. Find them, bring them, and then…then you will be allowed to orgasm. As were all our friends last night.

All our friends. They had been fucked by me, until I had been fucked by them, and the transition had been made. Now I was woman.

"But I want to change back?"

"And you can. Just tell Count Dacian. He will send you to the far dungeon and you may experience all that pain again. And you will change back."

At that moment I heard a sound. I turned, and Count Dacian was descending the stairs. Black suit in black cloak. Shiny, slicked back hair. A glimmer deep in his whiteless eyes. He knew, and there was a great, sly humor inside him.

"Good morning, Alexandria."

"I want to change back."

"Of course you do. And you may. Tonight if you wish."

He agreed too quickly, and then I saw what he hadn't said. All the pain. I would have to go through that again. I would have to be fucked by everybody, and then I would have to fuck them.

I didn't want that pain. There was no way I could experience that pain again.

And there was no way I could experience all that frustration.

Hiedi smiled and hugged my arm. "I know. There is no way you can go back through that…that…"

No. I couldn't. I couldn't face the pain. I would have to stay a woman.

"Look at the good side," said Count Dacian. "You will never be hungry again. You will not feel heat nor cold. And you may go to town as often as you wish and prey upon the people. Besides, you became a woman. That was your choice, and it couldn't have been a choice unless there was something in you that wanted to be a woman."

"Fuck men," I shivered. Inside, way back in my cranium, I was a man. I didn't want to fuck men. But I was a woman, and my body wanted men. But the fear in me, the homophobia…

Count Dacian read my mind. "You will get used to it. You will come to love it. And I will help you."

Of course he would, like he had helped Hiedi that first night.

"And you will come to love the delightful frustration that rules you, that drives you forward."

Oh, God. The frustration. I must have fucked a thousand people last night, but without cumming. I was unbelievably horny, and I knew it would only get worse. What terrible trick was this?"

"No trick. Just a different life. A different species, if you will."

I stared in horror at the wicked Count.

"Now, please enjoy yourself, and come Monday morning you should go to the inn and retrieve my note and cell phone."

I put my hands to my face, covered my eyes, and began to sob.

I was caught. Trapped. A woman forever. Or at least a very, very long time. I had a feeling I wouldn't be allowed to die until I had experienced the utmost in frustration and was capable of no more.

"Oh, Alexandria, it's okay!" Hiedi soothed me.

Count Dacian reached for my wrists. He was strong. Stronger than any human. He moved my arms down and stepped closely. He flicked out a snaky tongue and licked my tears. He drank my tears, and he murmured, "So delicious. So good."

END

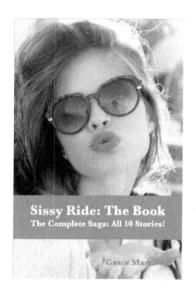

Sissy Ride: The Book!

A giant saga of feminization!
Check it out at…

https://gropperpress.wordpress.com

The Urban Hucow Farm

Urban Hucow farms feed the world!

PART ONE

With the fall of the United States came hunger. Grocery stores were empty, people roamed the streets looking for food. Hidden gardens became the order of the day. And a solution had to be found.

Wikispeedia

"Honey, I'm hungry!"

Jeffrey looked down sadly. "I'm sorry. I'm not much of a provider."

I looked at my husband of ten years. He was a large man. All the hamburgers and fries, all the potato chips and ice cream, he was a large man.

He was handsome, but bloated out to 300 pounds.

But, he had also been a good provider. A great provider. I was a little, uh, overweight myself. but a gal never tells, right?

We lived in a gated community, veddy expensive to live there, and we were somewhat safe from the people who roamed the streets looking for food, breaking into homes, looting and even murdering for a can of spaghetti.

"What are we going to do?"

"Well, there's Cannibalism."

I shivered. He was joking, but there were already stories on the news about people eating people.

"Actually, I was going through the garage and I found a can of Spam."

"Spam?"

"The other meat. Or something." He grinned.

"I think that's cats."

It was his turn to shiver. He loves cats, and ours had disappeared.

"We really have a can of Spam?"

"We do." He lifted a rectangular tin of the meat and grinned.

Like children at Christmas staring at presents we sat at the kitchen table and stared at the can.

It was blue with a hamburger on the front. It had a pop top. It contained…meat!

"We have to do this right," Marvin said. His jowls hung and he drooled unashamedly.

"Let's open a Coke."

He looked at me. "Do we dare?"

We dared, and I ran to the attic to get one of our last remaining Cokes. When we had last gone to the grocery store, a month before, the only thing they had was Coke. So we picked up a case. And would have picked up more if they had let us.

I returned to the kitchen and placed the can on the table. We stared at it hungrily. Two cans. Paradise. A taste of civilization. We wouldn't even have to boil water.

"What's in Spam?" I asked. "Where did it come from?"

Marvin took out his iPhone. Incredibly, with all the collapse, the government had mandated that the phone services, and other communication devices, be kept functioning. The better to get the bad news, I guess. We didn't even pay our bills and our phones kept working.

He pressed the side and asked, "What is Spam?"

Click. Whizz. Phhh. And it spoke: "Spam is Spiced Ham. The name stands for 'Special Processed American Meat. Many people are surprised to learn that Spam is not preservative laden. It actually has only six ingredients: pork with ham meat added, salt, water, potato starch, sugar, and sodium nitrite.

Marvin turned his phone down and tilted his head. "Pork with ham added?"

"Isn't that a bit redundant? Isn't ham actually pork?"

He asked his phone the difference we found out that ham comes from the thigh, and that pork comes from anywhere."

"Sort of like chicken nuggets," I quipped. "What part of the chicken is the nugget?"

We laughed, and took to staring at the metal containers in front of us.

"Well, Marsha," Marvin finally said. "I think we've anticipated enough. Would you like to do the honors?"

I pushed the Coke to him and pulled the Spam to me. We grinned, popped our tops, and shortly were spooning, sipping, and trading cans with every bite and gulp.

"Oh, my God!" Marvin sighed.

"Yes, there is a God!" I muttered.

We spooned, sipped sparingly, which was awful hard, and the golden Spam, and the Coke, disappeared.

We sat back and sighed. Marvin placed his chubby hands on his belly and moaned.

I looked at him. "Are you saying what I think you're saying?"

He grinned. "After a good meal…"

"…you want sex."

His smiled broadened.

"Oh, my God."

He wanted sex, food did that to him. But I had been so hungry these past few weeks, I was even starting to lose weight, that I didn't want sex."

"Do we have to?" I whined.

"Hey! Wifely duties, woman! Now snap to it! Get those clothes off and get on all fours."

That was another thing. Marvin absolutely loved doggy style. I didn't.

He claimed he could get extra penetration, which was correct because missionary caused our bellies to get in the way. Doggy style didn't. Only one belly got in the way then.

But then I had to support his weight, and, as I said, Marvin is a big boy.

"Marvin! I can't! I'm too weak."

"You just had a meal," he complained. He was leaning across the table, a gleam in his eyes.

I sighed. I did love him, and I was the wife. But... "Okay, sex. But we do it my way."

His eyebrows lowered a bit. "And what way is that."

"I'll give you a blow job."

He cocked his head. "A blow job? I can have that."

"Okay."

"All right."

We got up and walked up the stairs. I walked, because I had lost more weight than him. He...well, I have to say it, he waddled.

We entered our bedroom and began taking off our clothes.

"No foreplay?" I asked.

"We can if you want," he replied.

I sighed. "No, let's get this over with. Lay down."

He flopped on the bed, and the bed groaned. One of these days that bed was going to collapse under him.

I got him to scoot back a bit, and knelt between his legs.

Marvin was large, and I pushed his belly up and pulled his weenie out. He actually had a pretty good sized dick. In fact, when we had met I was astounded at how big it was, but that was a big dick on a smaller body. With the increase of bulk his dick just looked smaller.

Whatever, it was still a mouthful.

I placed my lips around the head and began swirling my tongue around it.

He groaned.

I stroked his shaft, up and down, and felt the veins.

He moaned.

I hefted his balls, squeezed and slapped them.

"Oh, baby!" he wheezed.

I took his dick in as far as I could, I sucked and slurped and worked him.

Fortunately for me, Marvin is a quick cummer. That used to bother me, but as he became larger it bothered me less.

Finally, he began to jerk, and his dick shot semen into my mouth.

He came hard, and it shot down my throat, and then I had to swallow quickly. I gulped and gulped, and that's when it hit me.

Semen.

Calcium, citrate, fructose, glucose, lactic Acid, magnesium, potassium, protein, zinc. 300,000,000 sperm. That's three hundred MILLION!

I swallowed.

And smiled.

I had just discovered another food source.

And, as if that wasn't enough, on the very next day the government announced mass distribution of soy beans.

Talk about nefarious.

But…one does what one has to to survive.

We came downstairs, Marvin happy and feeling that lazy feeling that comes after a cum.

Me feeling happy and a bit energized. I had just had a shot of protein. And other stuff.

Marvin went into the den to take a nap.

I went in to the computer room and started researching.

Sperm has the protein of an egg, the vitamin C of an orange, lots of B-12, enzymes, and all sorts of other stuff.

It is excellent as a cosmetic and an anti-aging food.

Wow. I closed the computer and thought about it.

I had just had breakfast, in a manner of speaking. The only problem was that it was a small breakfast.

The Spam had gone a long way, but the extra kick of the semen had really 'provided the juice.' But I had only had a teaspoon of the stuff.

Hmm. I did the math.

If I needed two eggs for every meal, and two oranges, not to mention a double helping of vitamins and minerals, I was going to have to suck Marvin off at least six times a day. Forty-two times a week.

Not likely.

Marvin was good for three or four times a week. And that was when he was in the best of shape. Now he was probably good for one or two times a week.

I needed Marvin to produce more sperm.

I headed back up to the bedroom. It was time to make myself over.

I walked down the stairs. Marvin was out in the garage. We had hooked up lamps and were growing food out there. It wasn't much food, but we couldn't grow it outside or our garden would get ransacked. Even inside a gated community there were people who would raid our veggies if we grew them outside.

Marvin glanced up, looked back down, then straightened up and looked at me.

I was wearing a corset, and looked about 20 pounders lighter. Mind you, I wasn't wasp waisted, yet, but it was a good start. My hair was fresh washed and conditioned, it was long and silky, shiny, gold in the sun.

The corset had pushed up my boobs, which were big anyway, and I was, in a word, stacked. My boobs would definitely walk into a room before I did.

I was wearing a thin dress, silky, and everything was showing. The fact that I was a little overweight made my pussy show. I had a real 'monkey knuckle,' or 'camel's toe,' or whatever men called it.

I was made up, with smoky eyes and the reddest lips. One look at my red lips and a man would catch fire.

"Fuck," said Marvin, wiping sweat off his fatty forehead. "I just fucked you, and damned if you're not making me want to again."

"As soon as you're regenerated I'll haul your ashes al-l-l the way to the dump."

He blinked. He wasn't used to sexy talk. Then he laughed.

"I'm ready now."

I pushed him away with hands to his bulgy chest. "Not for a couple of days, big boy. I have to recover from this morning."

"But I didn't…it was oral!"

"That's okay. You still need to build up your sperm count. Right?"

"Well, uh…"

"So I'm going to take a walk."

"I'll go with you."

"No, no. You stay here and rest. Build up the spermies."

"But…you can't go out like that!"

"I'll wear a coat."

Well, he wanted to, but I didn't want him to. I had plans which didn't include him. So I finally managed to make him understand that he needed to stay home and tend the garden.

He looked at the tiny, little tomatoes, he looked at me, a ripe tomato, and he sighed. But he agreed, and I was off.

I didn't take the car, couldn't spend the gas, so I simply walked down the sidewalk towards the gate. I made it to two houses before I took off my coat, and Jimmy Gatsby immediately called to me from his garage. "Hey, beautiful, where you going?"

I smiled and sauntered over to his open garage door.

"How's Tina?" I asked. I didn't want any complications for what I was planning.

"She left me."

"What?"

"She went home to her mother. She lives in the country and they grow lots of food out there."

"But she didn't…you didn't go with her?"

He shook his head. "We were fine as long as I was making money, but when the collapse came and my income dried up…"

"And when the pudding and ice cream dried up," I added.

"There's that," he nodded. Then he grinned. "So I'm footloose and fancy free, want to come see my etchings?"

We laughed, then I surprised him. "Sure."

He blinked. "Okay."

I could see the glee in him. A beautiful woman walks by, he gets to tap into it. Yeah, baby.

I followed him into the kitchen, then we sat down in the living room.

"So how are you and Marvin doing?"

"We're okay, we don't seem to be able to get the garden thing going," I shrugged.

"Yeah. I lost my green thumb during the war."

"You know, I would do almost anything for a…a can of something."

I said it directly.

He hesitated, he was obviously weighing the fact that I was married. His horniness won out. "Anything?"

"Hell, I would even suck your dick. I'm just so hungry."

He paused for a long minute. I think he was comparing can versus blow job. "I might have…maybe…a can of soup."

"Campbells?"

"Yes."

He eyed me, waited for me to say 'it's all a joke,' or to deliver.

"I would blow your cock, suck it until it runs dry, if you would give me a can of Campbell's soup.

He stood up, walked out of the room. I heard him climbing the stairs, then I heard him descending. He walked into the room, and he was holding a red can.

Beenie Weenie. Oh, fuck. My favorite.

"Jimmy," I said. "Take your pants down and prepare to forget about your wife."

"That bitch?" he grinned, his buckle came undone, his pants dropped. He was commando and his penis stuck out like a sword.

I had not seen many men's penises in my life. I had only had two before fucking my husband, and I had only touched lips to one of those.

Of course Marvin had encouraged me to learn to give blow jobs, and I had practiced on him till I was white in the face. Literally.

I tossed a cushion on the floor and knelt in front of Jimmy. The one-eyed snake stared back at me.

It was not big, probably average, and it tilted up slightly. The veins weren't big throbbers, but when I put my hands on it I could feel a strong pulsing.

I reached under and cupped a ball.

He groaned.

The ball felt full, to say the least.

"How long?" I asked.

"Two weeks."

"Two weeks without. You probably would have died if I hadn't come along."

"Definitely," he groaned as I stroked his shaft.

"Well, your troubles are over." I kissed his dick, let my lips slid around the knob, began deep throating him.

That's right. I can deep throat.

I can only half deep throat Marvin, but then he's big. An average sized dick I could deep throat.

Jimmy gasped as my lips hit his pubic area. I left the imprint of my lips in a circle around the base of his cock.

He shaved, and I was glad. I encourage all men to shave. Nothing is worse than picking hairs from your teeth.

Slowly I ran my hand up and down. I licked the under part of his cock. I twisted the knob with my hands, my saliva making it slide extra juicy.

"Oh, fuck," Jimmy muttered. I could tell he was close. Two weeks without? Any man would be close. And that was good. I didn't want to work hard for this. I had plans, and they included keeping my lips in working order.

I began bobbing my head, working my hand, and his knees suddenly buckled and he began shooting.

Squirt, squirt, squirt. Down my eager throat his vitamins and minerals went. One more egg, one more orange. Oh, yes.

When he was done I wanted to keep sucking, but I knew that, at a certain point, it would become painful. I wanted him to remember only the pleasure.

I let him go, smacked my lips, and pushed him back on the couch. I rolled back and up and sat in a chair.

"Woo!" He said.

We stared at each other and grinned.

"Thank you," he said.

"You're welcome."

"If I can find another can of soup...?"

Leave the red flag on your mail box up. I may not be able to service you quickly, but I'll get there."

"You got it." He smiled, then he frowned a bit.

"What?"

"Do you want...I've got a lot of Christa's stuff upstairs. I was just going to throw it away. Do you want it?"

Oh, Lord. Christa was about my size. Had great, expensive tastes. Did I want it? When I had to keep myself beautiful if I was going to hand out a half dozen blow jobs a day? You fuckin' A I want it!

"Sure," I said, acting nonchalant.

We went upstairs, and I hit the bonanza. She had dresses, shoes, even lingerie. I tried a couple of things on, not worrying about whether Jimmy saw my naked form—after all, it just served to accelerate his return to horny.

"Are you sure? I can use a lot of this stuff."

"Sure. Save me a trip to the dump."

I looked at her vanity. "How about the make up?"

"Be my guest."

So I forwent another meal and focused on toting a half a dozen boxes over to my house.

Marvin came out of the garage and looked at my goodies. "Where'd you get that?"

"Jimmy Gatsby, down the street. His wife left him and he's throwing it out."

"Huh!" he went back to the garden.

I finished moving the dresses and stuff, then looked at the can of soup.

Beenie Weenie. OMG! I took it upstairs and hid it in my clothes closet. I full intended to bring it out the next day, share it with Marvin, maybe with another Coke. That was not to be , however.

I went out again, it was now late afternoon, and I had to leave the community to find my next meal. I found it however, and brought home a can of Spaghetti-eos.

Gah.

But, what the hell. Beggars can't be choosers. At least, so I thought at the time.

I returned home before dark with the Spaghetti eos in my purse and a stomach full of gism. And a smile on my face.

I was good looking, and I was surviving. Both Jimmy and the man I had found outside the community had been very appreciative. And both wanted return performances.

It looked like Marvin and I were going to make it after all.

Then tomorrow hit, and the world changed.

"Oh, my God!" Marvin came charging out to the patio. "Food! They're giving us food!"

I looked up from the lawn chair where I was soaking up the rays. "Who is?"

"The government," I stood up and looked at his iphone.

GOVERNMENT SHIPS SOY!

The federal government has unveiled plans to immediately distribute Soy beans. These delicious beans are easy to grow and the government has secured purchases from...

I took the phone from his hands and stared at it.

"Food!" I gasped. "We're going to get real food!"

"We'll have to cook it ourselves, but the newsheads say bags of the beans will be distributed from the fire stations of every city. Look at the pictures!"

I stared at photos of trains filled with bags of soy beans.

"There's other food, too, but soy is the main staple. Apparently Soy is rich with vitamins and..."

He blathered on, and my head spun.

I had two cans upstairs, and was about to go out and find some more. Should I?

And I realized, right away, that I should.

Soy might be good, but I needed that unique protein that was in sperm. The eggs and the oranges. Furthermore...I liked it. I liked going out and finding out about men's dicks. I liked feeling them, and sucking them. I liked the way their legs gave way. And I actually liked the taste of semen.

Sure, sometimes it was bitter, but I could get used to that. Many times it was also sweet. I think it sort of depended on what men ate.

And I wondered what the taste would be like when all the men were sucking down the soy. Probably like soy sauce, and I could handle that.

So I celebrated with Marvin, and then went out.

It was late, so I intended to share a can with him when I got back.

I met two men in the gated community who had cans. One was a black fellow with a giant pickle for a schlong. And when he came it was two meals. The other fellow was older and I had to work at it, and then his semen was bitter.

Ah, well.

Then I met a fellow just outside the community, and he was a bonanza. He paid me a can of peaches, then asked if he could have a freebie for every man he brought me?

42

We finally agree on a freebie for every three men, and parted on a smile.

My business was building.

But, when I came home Marvin was sleeping. And I was a little tired, too. Being on my knees so much, you know. So I went up to bed and slept right through to dinner.

For dinner Marvin fixed a big salad. Probably the whole crop of tiny tomatoes and withered radishes and saggy leaves of Kale. But it was dinner, so I held off on the Beenie Weenie. Tomorrow was another day. Except the next day we went downtown and picked up our first bag of soy beans. Fifty pounds of the pellets. We returned home, and had soy every day for a week, and by then several things had happened.

First, I had a business. In fact, I was so busy on my knees that I didn't even want to suck Marvin off.

Second, Marvin was so busy concocting soy bean dishes he wasn't interested in getting a blow job.

Well, that was a first. Even at his chubbiest my hubby always liked getting his jackhammer jacked. I mean, what's up with that? Eh?"

Third, I noticed a strange phenomena.

I had been eating almost nothing but sperm, and I was losing weight. Yes, I was eating a lot of sperm, but there's not a lot of fat in sperm. It's all protein. And a protein rich diet, especially taken a teaspoon at a time, was making me skinnier. Thank God my boobs weren't getting skinnier. I had a couple of customers who held out, until I told them they could suck my tits. There's something about tits that drives a man wild.

But Marvin was putting on weight.

A week of soy and he was getting heavier. And not just heavier, but fatter. Real fatter.

It was time to do some research, so I powered up the computer and began looking up soy.

Oh, fuck. Soy beans had fat. I read further…but it was good fat. And a person shouldn't gain weight on a diet of soy.

So why was Marvin gaining weight?

I researched further, and I found it.

Estrogen.

Both men and women need estrogen and testosterone. Men need more testosterone, and women need more estrogen. But what happened when men ingested too much estrogen? They began to change. Sexually.

In horror I stared at the articles I was reading.

No, the fat was okay, but the estrogen was creating a different body. Exercise could cure it, bu tI knew Marvin wasn't about to hit the gym. If the gyms were even open. In fact, he was moving less and less.

And estrogen resulted in low libido and muscle mass, mood

changes, reduced energy levels, all of which explained why Marvin didn't feel like getting sucked off.

Well, sucking him off didn't bother me. After all, I had customers out the door.

But...with no exercise the fat wouldn't burn off, wouldn't redistribute properly, and he would get big breasts.

I decided to talk to Marvin, and I made a mistake. I decided not to just talk to him, but to come clean about what I had been doing.

That night, after dinner, I sat him down. I started easy like. "Marvin, you're getting too fat."

A hurt expression drifted across his face.

"You need to exercise."

"Aw, but I don't have the energy to exercise!"

He was caught in that old catch 22. He needed energy to exercise, the exercise took too much energy.

I went right into the next subject. "Marvin, I've been out giving blow jobs."

"WHAT?"

"Now calm down. It's a source of protein. I need the protein, and that means I need to eat less, and that leaves more for you."

Well, he hit the roof. We had our first major fight ever. He screamed and he cried. He stomped up and down so much I was afraid he was going to break the house.

But I held my ground.

"A blow job is not like fucking. I am NOT being untrue to you."

"But other men are putting their dicks in your mouth!"

"And feeding me."

"And that's why you've been waking around in all these sexy dresses! Your face all made up! So you can cheat on me!"

"I am not cheating on you!"

"Do you kiss any of these men?"

I stopped for a second, then blurted, "Not very often."

"Ah ha! Ah ha!"

Oh, man, we went around and around. And I got so pissed off that I didn't even tell him about the cans of stuff I was collecting. I mean, if he was going to treat me that way, have so little understanding, I wasn't going to tell him anything!

And, we went to bed angry.

Lumps on each side of the bed. Refusing to talk.

It's bad to go to bed angry, so I had weird dreams, dreams that I couldn't remember, but which upset me.

Then I woke up.

Marvin wasn't in bed.

I tiptoed downstairs, and heard him crying on the couch. He was just sitting there, his head in his hands, and crying.

"Marvin, I'm sorry," I sat next to him and put my arm around him. He was so large it didn't go very far around him. "It's just that I got so hungry, and we...I sucked you off last week, and I got the idea."

He sniffled and put his head against my shoulder.

"But...but I can't bear the thought of you with another man."

I sat there, him leaning against me, sniffling and snorting, and thought about it.

In a way, I wasn't cheating. My hole was my own to give out as I wished, and I didn't wish to give it to anybody but Marvin.

In a way...I was. I was being with other men. And, as Marvin had noted, I was kissing them, and letting them feel and even suck my tits. That was an act of intimacy. Especially as I used that act to excite the men into giving me more sperm.

But...I needed food. I needed the nourishment that sperm gave me. Even if I hadn't liked it, I needed it. But I did like it. I liked slurping on a man's cock until it exploded. I liked the feeling when they released into me.

"You should try it."

He blinked. And, tell the truth, I don't even know where that came from. But it come, and I wasn't about to pull it back.

"Sucking dick?"

I thought wildly. I had said something, and it was wrong, but there was something underneath it.

"No. You should try packaging your semen, selling it to women as food. Trading it for cans.

He stared at me like I was insane.

But I wasn't, and things were borning in my mind.

Semen packaged for food. We could mix it with soy, make super soy. The taste would...depending, be labeled as sweet or tangy.

And I knew women would buy it.

Women are always into the latest health food. They always want the latest and greatest. They liked the gimmicks.

They would buy it.

But first I had to figure out how to produce and package. And then I would have to get a distribution network. And it had to be kept very, very secret. This was commerce. I couldn't exactly go get a patent. But I had to keep my 'trade secrets' truly secret.

Still, there was a way. And I would find it.

With that in mind I left Marvin to wallow on the couch, to cry out the hormones his soy diet, his estrogen diet, was creating. I headed to the computer room and began researching.

PART TWO

"Would you like a shot of pure protein?"

Cindi Lawson looked at me. I was holding a little bottle. It was actually a bottle used for baby food. I had traded a blow job for it, and now it was being re-used. It was filled with a mix of Marvin's sperm and soy beans.

"What is it?"

"It's milk and soy. Would you like to trade for a can?"

She did, and I walked away with a can of chili, and she was smacking her lips and smiling.

I had jacked Marvin off, mixed his seed with soy, and the result was a tasty treat packed with protein. Soy, it appeared, resulted in sweet sperm.

And the great thing about this was that I had sucked Cindi's husband off the night before. He gives his sperm and a can to me, and I give her Marvin's sperm and she gives me a can. Ironic, eh?

I returned home and placed the chili in front of Marvin.

Oh, God, he disappeared into that can, and here's the funny thing: Soy made you fat, but it never really filled you up. By that I mean it was filling, but it didn't provide enough of the vitamins and nutrients that a man needed.

He finished the can and was actually gasping. He begged, "Please. Milk me. Do this again."

I smiled. Marvin had been a problem, with his whining about me being untrue, but I had found a solution. He was willing to be milked and his seed sold. And if somebody else was going to be eating his semen, how could he complain about me eating somebody else's semen?

"Marvin, I can milk you, but…we have a couple of problems."

"What's that?" He looked at me with big eyes.

I was truly surprised at how he was changing. His body was getting bigger. His thighs were truly 'thunder thighs,' and his breasts….they were so big they looked like tits.

"Well, it's awkward for me. I get very tired of either being on my knees and fighting your belly," he knew that that big roll of flab was overflowing more and more, "and while the doggy position is fine, I still have to be on my knees."

"Oh," he looked so sad. "Does that mean you're not going to milk me anymore?

"No, no. But we need to build you a milking station."

"A milking station?"

"Yes. So you'll be raised up enough for me to get behind you and not have to wear out my knees. It's going to be good for you, too. You don't have to get all the way down on the bed, and then get up again. You just walk into the milking station, bend into position, and I'll take care of the rest."

He frowned, and there was so much fat on his pudgy face that his cheeks came forward and his nose went back. I thought that was sort of cute. I mean, he didn't have a cow face, but, sort of a piggy face.

"Who's going to build this thing for you?"

"Jimmy Gatsby said he'll help."

"Is he one of your customers?"

"That doesn't matter." I glared at him. "I'm just trying to make your life easier, and get you more food! And don't tell me you don't like it when I stick a finger up your ass and help you cum!"

"Oh, sorry." funny, it sounded like his voice was changing.

"So how about it."

"I guess so."

So Jimmy Gatsby traded a little handyman work for two blowjobs and a can of Coke. But it was a good trade, I had a feeling Marvin was going to be, pardon the expression, a 'cash cow.'

While Jimmy pounded and hammered in the garage—we had finally given up on the vegetable garden crap—I was out on the street. And I had a bad experience.

It was a fellow I hadn't met before, but he came recommended. But recommendations don't mean much. They just mean that somebody knows somebody. There's no character reference or Human Resources to check with.

And, I didn't like him, but it was a job, and I proceeded to give him a good blow.

Half way through he grabbed my hair, hard, and fucked my face.

"Hey!" I garbled.

"Shut up, bitch!"

And I knew he was going to fuck my face, then probably slap me around, and not even pay me. Fucking asshole.

So I did the only thing a girl can do. I grabbed his nuts and I...
PULLED!

Oh, Lord, he dropped so fast he hit his chin on the ground. He was already out of it, holding his nuts, but I couldn't help myself. I stood up and kicked him in the face. That actually hurt me more than him, the pointy toes of high heels look dangerous, but it is all show. The toes collapsed and I near broke a toe on him. So I reached into my purse, took out a can and slapped him on the temple with it.

Lucky boy, he went unconscious and stopped feeling the pain in his balls. Heh.

I found two cans in his pockets, took them both, and walked away. I figured he owed me one can for the blow job, and one can for the semen he hadn't given me.

But from that day on I went armed. And I mean really armed. I was quite a sight. I would wear a skin tight, red dress, my boobs big and quaking, and a big, old hunting knife strapped around my now svelte waist. And, if that wasn't enough, I had a pistol strapped to my ankle. I couldn't run with a pistol on my ankle, but I wouldn't have to because I drilled on how to quick draw that pistol while in a kneeling position.

But here's the funny thing: wearing all that armament actually brought me in more business. It seems like men like a blow job that's a little dangerous.

In fact, one guy, who was a little slow, I pulled the knife and held it under his balls and said, "Your cum or your testicles."

He came so fast and quick it went down my throat without me even tasting him.

And, he became a repeat customer, and he always tried to hold back until I pulled out the knife and threatened him.

Men. Huh!

"Just walk in there," I said.

Marvin climbed a couple of steps and waddled into the chute, then knelt on a soft cushion. He lowered himself and his big bulk was in the doggy style.

I walked around the contraption and nodded. "Nice." His big butt was elevated and his chest hung down. His pecs looked more and more like boobs every day, and they hung down like big milk sacs.

"It feels comfortable," Marvin remarked. "More comfortable than my easy chair. Easier on my back, too."

"Would you like to try it out?"

"Sure."

I moved in behind him I reached between his legs, and it didn't work.

I walked around to the side and was able to reach his cock easier. I placed a bowl under him, sat down on a stool, and began stroking him.

"Oh, God," he muttered. "This is so comfortable."

I kept eyeing his tits, and, finally, I couldn't help myself. I reached under the station and grabbed one of his tits.

"Oooh!" he moaned.

I massaged his tits, jacked his cock, and it was very comfortable for me, too.

After a minute he squirted.

"Oh, yeah!" He gave a big, pudgy-faced smile.

"Okay, big boy," I stood up and slapped his rump.

"You're done?"

"I got the milk. Yeah, I'm done."

"But you only massaged one side!"

I blinked. "Really?"

"Yeah. It felt so good. Can you do the other one?"

The other tit. My God.

So I did. I went to the front of him, sat on a stool with my pussy right in his face, and massaged his tits.

He moaned and groaned, and...sniffed.

"Are you smelling my pussy?"

"Yeah," he giggled.

I had to laugh. What a horn dog. He looked like a hucow, but he was a horn dog. But, then, aren't all hucows horn dogs? Or the other way around?

So we were set. I was getting my semen diet. We were getting lots of cans and the world was fine and dandy! Except...

"Marsha?"

"Hey, Molly. How's it going?"

We talked, a little chit chat, then she forged ahead.

"How do you stay so...sexy? I hate that soy stuff, and I'm starving. My tits are getting smaller. And what's worse, my Joe is getting fatter! He really likes that soy stuff."

Now, you can see where this was going.

I had known Molly for years, and we were friends, and I sat her down and told her the facts of life. When I was done she just sat there. Stunned.

"You trade blow jobs for cans. You get fed twice."

"Yep."

"And you trade Marvin's semen for cans.

"You got it."

"But...I don't..."

I waited. I sort of knew what was going to happen.

"Can I...could you have Joe, my hubbie, do something like that?"

Huh. I thought she was going to ask for herself.

"Sure."

It always amazes me, that people would want to work for somebody else, which meant somebody else was going to get part of their profits, instead of working for themselves. But there it was. She was renting her husband out, and talking about going and giving blow jobs and paying me for the leads. That's okay by me.

So I started training her on how to give blow jobs, and I had Jimmy build another stall for Molly's husband to occupy. And here's the funny thing: I thought Marvin would object, but he actually looked forward to the company.

He was spending more time in the stall these days, it was just so much more comfortable than waddling around, trying to get up the stairs, and he had moved a TV out to the garage and spent a lot of time just laying in the stall and watching Fox News.

So the idea of having somebody next to him, being able to discuss the news of the day and being able to cuss out those damned Democrats...Joe was in, pardon the phrase, 'hog heaven.'

But...there was one other problem. I wasn't getting fucked. I was sucking cock like a madwoman, and I was milking Marvin, and now Joe —and, I was horny.

There, I said it.

I was horny, my poontang hadn't been clanged. My pussy hadn't meowed. My hole hadn't been filled.

All Marvin's squirts had gone for commerce, for cans, and I wasn't getting my depths plumbed.

And, let's face it, got to be honest, Marvin was so large now that I was afraid of him being on top of me. Missionary was totally out of the question. And if his arms gave way during a doggy style session, and he fell on me, well, I would be a Marsha pancake.

So I was horny. I had no prospects with Marvin, and I had a potential stud, though not with a big dick, in Jimmy.

And, here comes the shock of shocks. I went out to the garage, turned off Fox News, and sat down in front of Marvin.

"Hi, honey. Do you mind? Tucker Carlson was just going to interview Joe Biden."

"I'll turn it back on in a second."

He craned his head to the side and tried to look around me. The screen was blank, but he still tried.

"Marvin, you haven't been satisfying me sexually."

"Oh," he tried to look around the other side of me.

"So I'm going to fuck Jimmy Gatsby."

"Oh, okay. Could you turn the TV back on?"

I smiled, turned the TV back on, and left. Left right out of the house, down the street, into Jimmy's house, up the stairs, got rid of my clothes, and hopped into the sack.

ZOWIE!

Jimmy didn't like soy, and it turned out that he had his own business. He arranged for the smuggling of aliens back across the border.

That's right, when the country collapsed all those illegal aliens suddenly wanted to go home. They tried to get to the border, but the buses weren't reliable, the trains were very strict in not letting people ride for free, and the immigrants were getting caught.

Enter Jimmy. One or twice a week he would load up a small truck with a few dozen aliens, pack them in like cattle, and take them down to the border. Once there they could simply walk across the border.

So Jimmy had a good business, and lots of cans, and he could afford to hate soy. The result was that he was in prime shape. He ate enough to have energy to work out, and he worked out. A lot.

So I divested myself of clothes, and he ripped his off. Literally ripped them off, he was that strong, and he took me in his arms.

I munched on his lips, chewed on his mouth, and it was a delight. He was firm, not fat laden, and he was dedicated.

He lifted me up and laid me on the bed, then he really went to work. He crawled beneath my legs and began giving me a tongue job like no other. He might have a short dick (well, average sized), but he had a lo-o-ong tongue!

Man, he inserted that wiggly into my depths and made me cry 'Hallelujah!' He lapped at my labia, clamped on to my clit, and by the time he slithered up my body I was feeling like a hundred pounds of jello. Hot jello.

He put his hands on my chest, fondled my boobs, and began sucking my nipples. All the time his dick was getting closer and closer. Finally, me turning into a steamy, sopping mess, he inserted that bad boy.

"Oh...fuck!" I whispered.

He drove into me, almost lazily. The fact was he knew that he had done his duty with foreplay, and I was a cooked goose. My body properly primed, his touch electrified me. I could feel sensations shooting through me. My breasts felt like they were on fire. My lips were delightfully numb from his lips. And now my pussy was finally filled.

No, not big like Marvin, but the heat of the meat plus the angle of the dangle...over the mass of the ass...it all equals the sum of the cum.

Within minutes I was shuddering and jerking. My pussy literally exploded. My mind shattered. I lived in those high clouds reserved for Greek Gods.

And, Joe let loose. And I'm sorry I didn't have a bottle to catch his cum. He was always a big cummer, but cumming inside me, he was a MONSTER cummer!

Finally, we rolled apart, lay on our backs and looked up.

"Crap. That was better than any blow job."

"Honey," I said. "I think we just graduated. If you want to pay me for fucks instead of blow jobs, I'm okay with that."

He smiled. "Excellent. Now that I've tasted nirvana I don't want to go back to purgatory.

"My blow jobs were purgatory?" I laughed and swatted him.

He caught my arm and rolled over me. He looked down on me. Our eyes met and we were really in synch. He said, "You want another cow for your business?"

Ka-ching! Money.

"Who?"

"I've got a cousin. She's a little…well, let's just say that she likes her soy. It's not that she can't get a job, even in these times you can get jobs, but…she doesn't want a job. She just wants to sit on her ass all day and read fashion magazines and watch the cooking channel."

"Hmmm." I considered, and Jimmy gave me the time. Except for a few nibbles at my highly energized nipples.

"Stop that!" I swatted his head gently. He laughed and waited.

"Okay, I can, but we have problems."

"No problem too big."

"I don't want to put a woman cow in with the men."

"Why not?"

"You put men and women together and there's always trouble. Next thing you know they'll want to diddle each other, even get married."

"We could set up in my garage. I'll build another stall, and you can manage both garages. I can't because I've got my own business."

We were lost in our own thoughts then. Finally, I stuck up my hand. "Shake. Let's seal the deal."

Jimmy kissed me, then, breathing hard, he whispered, "Let's fuck to seal the deal."

And damned if we didn't.

The girl's name was Nancy Pelosi. Just like on TV, and I was glad I hadn't put her in with Marvin and Joe. They would have ganged her quick. She had no politics, but her name was bad enough.

And she was good. She laid down quick and we suddenly had men lined up out the door, down the block and out the gate.

Hucows were a new thing. Before the country collapsed only weirdos had, or were, hucows. But now that 'normal' was gone, it turned out that *everybody* loved hucows. And everybody wanted to own one, or be one.

So Jimmy built another stall, this one in his garage, and with a few modifications.

With this stall we arranged for Nancy's pussy to be raised up. And her head.

That's right, she could take it from both ends. And then some.

After a week of work she waddled out of her stall and came down the street and knocked on the door.

"Hey, Nancy. How's it going."

"Pretty good. It's really neat to be loved, like, all the time."

"So what can I do for you?"

"I just wanted to know if you charged double for my asshole."

"What?"

"Yeah. Guy today didn't want my pussy. He was nice enough, told me so, even asked, and that's fine with me. Any port in a storm, right?"

Now this was a new one on me, and it led to some interesting little developments.

I put a sign over her stall.

One can for blow job.
Two cans for pussy.
Three cans for asshole.

Man, business picked up all over again. A lot of guys were dying to explore assholes. Their wives weren't too friendly to the idea, and, only three cans, why not?

And that led to another interesting conversation.

Knock knock.

I opened the door. It was one of my customers, a big, black fellow name Irwin.

"Hi Irwin. I didn't expect you until tomorrow."

He hemmed and hawed, was embarrassed, and I finally said, "Spit it out, Irwin."

"Well, uh, you got the girl putting out with all three holes."

"I do. Did you want some asshole this week?"

"Well, uh...how about the guys you got over in the other garage?"

I shut down for a moment over that one. "What do you mean?"

"Well, the girl don't mind, do the guys? Would any of them be prone to giving blow jobs? Or getting fucked in the ass?"

"Have a seat, Irwin. I'll go ask them."

Marvin said he'd think about it.

Joe, however, liked the idea.

So I went back and told Irwin, and he grinned a huge grin, like to have split his face. "How much for Joe's ass?"

"Three cans." Hey, that's what I was charging for the girl's asshole.

He paid it eagerly and couldn't wait to go out and collect his 'goods.'

While he was pumping away, and while Joe was moaning, and while Marvin was looking at Joe and wondering out what he was missing out on, I put some more signs up.

Over Joe I put.

One can for blow job.
Three cans for asshole.

I went around to Marvin. "You want to try this?"

"What's Joe get paid?"

I knew he didn't care about the pay, he was interested in the way Joe was groaning and moaning.

Then disaster, sort of, hit.

"Oh, shit! I'm cumming!" Joe yelled.

"Oh, crap!"I blurted. Irwin must have hit the prostate, and there went Joe's quota of semen. I started to the rear to see the damage, and Marvin yelled after me. "Yes! I want to try it!"

I looked under Joe's big belly and, sure enough, semen was dribbling out of his cock. A LOT of semen.

And then, while I was trying to figure out how much I had lost in profit, Irwin grunted and yelled. Fuck! I'm cumming!"

I was looking under Joe's belly, could barely see the tip of his cock, and suddenly a big gush of squirtem flowed down over his dick. A LOT of squirtem.

"Holy crap!" I muttered. That was two days worth of cum. Maybe three. I had some thinking to do.

I had to look into prostate massages, maybe some sort of low level cattle prod for the men to make them cum more.

And, I had some advertising to do.

I had four cows—another girl had come to my door and asked for a job—and I had to collect semen from the guys, Sell their asses and mouths, and I had to sell mouths, cunts and assholes for the girls.

I had a lot of customers, but I needed more. Especially since both of the girls said they had friends that wanted to work.

So I advertised. I put a sign up over my garage.

HUCOW URBAN FARM

Males   one can for blow job
          three cans for anal
Females one can for blow job
          two cans for pussy
          three cans for anal

At the bottom of the sign I wrote:

Male and female Hucows wanted

By the next week I had Jimmy build me a half dozen stalls, and I was negotiating for garages all through the community.

It was funny, all these rich people in a gated community were more than willing to park their cars outside and rent their garages for a few cans a week.

Within two weeks I had six male hucows and six female hucows, then the game changed.

I was raking in the cans, thinking about raking in Jimmy that night, and who should appear but...Irwin!

"Hey, Irwin? how's it squirting?"

"Pretty good, thanks, but I noticed you got a new product."

"I do?" I blinked.

"Yeah, that new girl, Debbie, she lactatin'.

"Lactating? Like...giving milk?"

"Yeah. And I was wondering..."

What he was wondering I had no idea, I was out the door and heading for the garage where Debbie, the lactator, was working. I had hired that girl for her holes, and she was putting out milk? WTF!

I went through the garage door and stopped in front of Debbie.

She was a nice looking girl, very fat tits, and now I knew why.

"You just gave birth?"

She was scared, and she blurted. "Please don't fire me!"

"I'm not going to, I just want to know if you have a kid."

"A long time ago. I gave birth, and I liked having milk flowing all the time, so I kept pumping and pumping, and sometimes my husband drinks it, but he was late for work this morning and didn't have time. So...I...I figured maybe..."

"How much milk do you put out?"

"Oh, about two gallons. If I milk a lot. I've got biguns," she stated proudly.

"Would you like to sell me your milk?"

"Sure!" she answered eagerly. "I been pouring it down the drain. You think people will buy my milk?"

"I do. Okay. I'll look into it, you keep dripping, and, uh, do you mind giving Irwin a free sample? He's one of our best customers."

"Irwin, the guy with the really big dong?"

"That's the one."

"Sure."

And there it was. Mother's milk. A new product. A couple of gallons a day, and I found that I could sell a lot. In fact, I started advertising for new mother's who were about to stop breast feeding their babies. It seemed like every new mother liked lactating, and wanted to turn a profit for their body's production.

Yippee!

A month passed, a good month. Jimmy and I had to rent a garage just to store our cans. He gave up his job, well, he had somebody driving for him, and he started bartering our cans for things we needed, things we needed to keep our Urban Hucow Farm going.

Which was good because I was having a lot of fun fucking.

I wasn't fucking him for love, I loved Marvin. I was fucking Jimmy for fun. We would just work all day, look at each other, and go relieve our brains out.

And, one day, it came to a head. Uh, no pun intended.

"Marsha?"

"Yeah, Jimmy?"

We were upstairs and he was pumping me like it was going out of style.

"Let's give the Hucows hormones."

"What do you mean?" I asked. He was taking me from behind and I reached down and grabbed his balls. He cupped my hanging breasts and I moaned.

"We can give the gals more hormones to produce milk. Supposed to make them hornier. And we can give the guys two kinds of hormones. One to increase sperm production, the other to make them lactate."

I stopped moving. Jerked off him and spun a round. I grabbed his almost spewing cock and held it while I spoke into his face.

"Are you saying we could double milk production? And even increase semen production?"

"Yes!" His voice squeaked because I was holding him rather tightly.

"Oh, fuck! We could double our can income!"

"Yes!" He squeaked. He was batting at my hands, but I was so excited I ignored him and just kept working figures in my head.

We had thirty girls and forty guys working. Each one was fucked four or five times a day. Blow jobs were down to two or three a day. I had ten girls that were lactating a couple of gallons a day, multiply by the number of cans per week, add in....the cost of soy beans...

"How much do the hormones cost?"

"Nothing."

"Nothing?" My turn to squeak.

"Government gives out hormones for free."

"Why would they do that?"

"You ever hear of the Georgia Guidestones?"

"What are they?"

"A bunch of big stone slabs somebody put up in Georgia. Something about a new world order, or something. Anyway, the government wants to reduce the population by 7 1/2 billion people. They only want 500 million people left. they figure that will be enough to feed them and keep them in fancy doodads. You know, work their factories and farms."

I stared at him.

"So the point is if they can give men hormones, get them to change into women, there won't be so much fucking and the population will reduce. Natural like.

I had reduced my grip, and all this time Jimmy had been pumping. Suddenly he came, just as I let go.

"Hey! No! Don't let go! Please…keep pumping!"

It was a perfectly ruined orgasm, and he stood there and dripped a couple of drops, then stared down at his partially pleased organ sadly.

I walked out of the room, down to the computer room, and fired it up.

I had been so busy with my own business that I had been ignored the world tragedy. Now I started looking.

Georgie Guidestones. Yep.

Free hormones. Yep.

Uh oh, other Hucow farms were starting up.

Crap! I had to register my business with the government. That meant taxes and regulations.

But that was okay. Better to make so much money that you had to pay taxes than not make money.

I turned to my original calculating. Gallons of milk per day. Pints of semen. How much did I need to cut the product.

Then I started thinking about the future.

Cosmetics. Natural, from grain fed Hucows.

Medicines.

Weight loss products.

Oh, my God, there was no end to the possibilities here.

I ran back up to the bedroom. Jimmy was sitting on the bed, pounding on his pud.

"What?" He looked up at me, caught, but not ashamed.

That's the thing about ruined orgasms. If you ruin it just right the guy can't cum for a while. And he's super horny and super desperate.

I pushed him back on the bed and his cock stuck up in the air. Red and dripping and wanting.

I sat on it.

"Fuck, Jimmy, order those hormones." I pumped him hard.

"We need to advertise more." I ground down on him and tilted my pelvis.

"We need more Hucows." I kissed him madly.

Jimmy loved it. From a ruined orgasm to a super fuck. He thrust up and rammed it into me.

"Fuck!" I pushed down hard.

We fought like that for a long minute. In and out, caught in our gleeful battle.

"We're going to be Hucow kings!" I bellowed. I twisted his nipples and he yelped, but now he was in the mood.

"I'll buy all the houses in the community." He grabbed my tits, slapped them. Squeezed them till I moaned.

"I'll make all the garages into pens and we'll pipe in soothing music." I reached behind me and twisted his balls.

"YIPE!"

I said, "I'll take out ads in the papers, on TV. We'll have a thousand head of Hucows! We'll raise our prices!"

He slapped my pussy and I started to cum. I bucked and shivered and my legs started to spasm. I managed to say, "We'll be the world's first Hucow millionaires!"

"Fuck, yes!"

I bent over him, my breasts bouncing as I squeezed everything I could out of my orgasm. Then I collapsed on him.

"Hey," he said, trying to fuck some more. "You didn't get me off."

I smiled into his chest, then braced my hands on his strong pecs and pushed up. I stated, "If you've got sperm, we need to sell it. Now get your ass down to the barn and get yourself milked.

He stared after me as I sauntered proudly out of the room.

And, damn. He actually did.

END

Full Length Books from Gropper Press

Jim Camden was a manly man, until the day he crossed his wife. Now he's in for a battle of the sexes, and if he loses...he has to dress like a woman for a week. But what he doesn't know is the depths of manipulation his wife will go to. Lois Camden, you see, is a woman about to break free, and if she has to step on her husband to do it...so be it. And Jim is about to learn that a woman unleashed is a man consumed.

<u>The Feminization Games</u>

I Made Him Love our Female Led Marriage

Chastity and feminization made him a better man

PART ONE

"Honey, we've got to talk."

I could see his shoulders raise up, his head go down. Whenever we heard those words on TV we knew some gal was going to talk some guy's head off. End of action and adventure and fun and stuff, beginning of…the bitch.

"I'm a little busy right now." He started to get up, and I grabbed his sleeve and tugged him back. He fell back on the sofa, would have tried to get up again, but I had him.

By the balls.

Not to be crude, but the way to a man's heart is not through his stomach. It is through his testicles. And penis. And his desire to squirt his little seed into a woman's womb.

Truth.

"Aw, come on. I need to…"

But his words were weak, especially since I was squeezing and fondling and loving his most precious body part.

I pushed him back and sat on him.

His erect penis poked up at me. The head pushed against his pants, against my pants, and rubbed against my slit.

Oh, yeah. This was the part of the argument that I liked.

"Randy, look around."

His eyes were wild, he was already trying to lift his pelvis into me, and he was liking this 'little talk.'

We were in our living room. Our apartment living room. With thin walls through which we could hear the neighbors talking. And making love at night. And even when their refrigerator door opened.

He looked at the threadbare couch, the prints on the walls, the lamp that had a burned out bulb.

"So?"

I unzipped him, reached in, and…stood up.

"Hey!" he yelped as he quickly leaped to his feet.

I dragged him into the kitchen. "Look at this place."

Thin pots and pans, all dented and burnt. Silverware from eight different sets. All manner of bowls.

"This is shabby!"

"It's for cooking! It's supposed to look like this!"

I dragged him into the bedroom. "Is this the way things are

supposed to be?"

The bed was saggy, a plague on our backs. Our pillows were old. There were stains on the drapes and even a hole in one wall.

"Wanna, make love?" he grinned, reaching for me.

I squeezed, and amorous thoughts gave way to excruciating pain.

"OW!" His knees buckled.

I threw him on the bed.

He lay on his back and looking up, and massaged his poor pecker. "You don't have to—"

I jumped on him. I sat on him, fitted my pussy, encased in jeans as it was, on his erect penis. "I've had enough of this squalor."

He stared up at me, sourly. He complained. "I work all day and—"

"And you don't bring home enough. You're happy in a go nowhere job, and our lives are wasting away."

"So why don't you go out and get a job."

His sore point. I stayed home and wrote books, and made a pittance on the net, and he went to work. Obviously, he wanted me to get a pick and shovel and work construction.

I ground down on him. He liked that. "I work all day long. And I will make money with my writing. But I shouldn't have to. The man is suppose to make the living. He is supposed to be the king of his castle, and the woman is supposed to be the queen!"

"But, I—"

"Does this look like a castle?"

"Well, I—"

"So we are going to make some changes around here."

"What kind of changes?" he asked, the picture of suspicion.

"If you can't be the king of your castle, then I will be the queeen of your castle."

I pushed back, slid off him. I began to undress.

His eyes opened, his second mind now fully engaged.

I took off my shirt and let him see my rather large bosoms. They were encased in a sturdy bra, but that was okay. Sometimes men are more turned on by what they can't see, what they can only imagine, than the real thing.

Silly men.

I slid out of my jeans.

"Oh, yeah," he muttered, his eyes locked on me like a heatseeker missile.

I stripped out of my panties and bra and walked into the bathroom.

He waited.

I stepped into the shower.

He had visions of me coming out all clean and laying down for him.

I scrubbed my body, shaved a few parts, and shampooed my hair.

When I came out of the shower he was naked, laying odalisque style, on his side with his head propped on one arm. His lascivious grin so wide it near split his face in two. His penis was erect and bouncing with lust.

I put on a pair of panties, and his eyes blinked.

I grabbed a fresh bra and slipped into it.

"Hey, what are you doing?"

I adjusted the bra. It was a half bra and my nips pointed outward. I put on a blouse and a skirt.

"I thought we were going to...to..."

"The queen doesn't spread her legs for peasants," I spoke haughtily, as if I was too good for him.

He swung around and sat, his hard penis all ready with nowhere to go.

"But...I thought...we were..."

I dried my hair, which effectively shut out his whining voice. When I was done and sitting at my make up table he started in again.

"Honey, I thought we were going to talk, and talk is a four letter word, and so is fuck, so I thought—"

While he blathered I primed and foundationed, did my eyes, and colored my lips.

Red. His favorite color. The color he would most like to see on his cock.

I stood up and looked in the wall mirror. "How do I look?" I asked, smoothing my skirt.

"Honey? What is going on?" He was on his feet now, standing next to me, and he was so horny his cock was actually dripping pre-cum.

Silly, horn dog man.

I turned to him.

"You might be happy with the way things are. You laugh and joke with your dim witted friends all day, and you drink cheap ass beer on the weekend and go all crazy for a bunch of politically incorrect millionaires who kick around the skin of a pig. I, however, am destined for better things.

"But, I don't..."

I put a finger to his lips. A sexy, red tipped finger. I reached down and grabbed his drippy friend.

"Honey, I am destined to be wined and dined, drive the best cars, live in a mansion. Are you?"

"Well, uh...yeah."

It was a weak acknowledgement. It was a word blurted out because he had to say something and he had no idea what to say.

"Good. Then wait up for me. The news at eleven."

I turned and walked out of the bedroom, out of the apartment, down the corridor and stairs, into the parking lot, into my car, and…zoom.

I had no doubt that Randy was stilling standing, gape mouthed, in the bedroom. Staring at his poor, deprived cock and wondering what had happened.

Silly man.

The meeting took place in a classroom in a local high school. There were a couple of teenagers lurking the halls, even this time of night, and they stared as I strolled passed. It was like they had never seen a big breasted, round bottomed, high heeled bitch.

Silly teenagers.

I found the room at the end fo the hall and walked in.

"Amy!" I was greeted by my friend, Susan. We air kissed and hugged and she began introducing me to her friends. She was the one who had gotten me all wound up about being the queen of my castle. After a couple of weeks of talking to her I was ready for a change. She had only been involved in this group for a month, but she already knew her way around.

I met the leader of the group, a few of the ladies, was handed a cup of coffee, with real beans! Not the MickyD swill, but hand picked beans lovingly ground and…and it was delicious.

"Okay, ladies. If you can have a seat."

The leader of the group was a middle-aged matron name of Barbara. I say middle-aged, but she presented herself with zest and elan. Her body was in a great shape, trim and slim and big boobed. Her face had few wrinkles and was perfectly made up. In short, she was the picture of a woman who ran her world the way it should be run.

"Welcome all, and let me get right to the point. Men have proved quite incompetent in ruling the world. How many of you have enough money? How many of you have your own homes? Drive the latest model of cars?"

She smiled a broad smile.

"Now before you chide yourself for pinching pennies and cutting out coupons, let me tell you that I was once where you are. I was victim to a husband who was happy being a go along sluggard. He had no real ambitions, he was happy to drive his ten year old beater, he scratched himself, drank beer on the weekends, and I, like a fool, put up with it.

"I lay down and spread my legs, rewarding the doofus for his lack of ambition, instead of grabbing the horse by the cock and smacking him on the head and letting him know who was boss."

I liked these words. They described my situation perfectly, and I could see other ladies nodding their heads and mumbling in agreement.

"So I took control. I chastised him. I feminized him, and I made him into a woman."

My jaw dropped. I thought I was going to learn things about making money. Her talk of spreading her legs was bold, but I could handle that. But…chastity? Feminization? That stuff was for perverts.

I looked around surreptitiously. I could see frowns, but nobody stood up and walked out. Okay. Let's see what else this gal had to say. She did present herself as a success, and success breeds. Maybe I should listen. I gave her my attention.

"The theory is quite simple. You, the ladies, want something better. They, the men, don't. So the obvious conclusion is that women are superior to men. We aren't willing to be part of a 'good, old boys' club.' We aren't willing to settle for the lesser things in life. And the solution is obvious.

"Now men can't really be women. At least, not without drugs and surgery. But they can become like women, and when they do they start to think like women, they start to appreciate the finer things in life. They start to want better houses and cars, to go to the best nightclubs, to live life as it was meant to be lived.

"So, the theory is simple, to elevate men we must take away their ability to spew their seed out willy nilly. This one thing reduces them from being so damned manly, and makes them, finally, able to listen.

"Then you must change their apparel, their manners, their very way of looking at life. Withholding sex gives you a lever that will move worlds…and it's fun!"

Next to me Susan let out her breath. I glanced at her, her eyes were shiny, her lips parted and she was breathing heavily.

Tell the truth, I was feeling the heat, too.

"So let's discuss this idea, of withholding sex, of chastity and feminization. Let's give you the tools to rule your world. Are you with me?"

There was a mutter of agreement that was sincere and intense.

"Okay, the first thing you have to do is…"

I got home at midnight. I was tired, it had been a long day, but I was elated.

Randy was up. Waiting for me. He was wearing a robe, and I knew he had nothing on underneath it.

Silly man.

"Where have you been?" He was on his feet instanter, and in my face.

Good. In my face is fine. Barbara had explained that the mistake most women make is not using their basic tools, and even deliberately and cruelly abusing them.

Or, in other word, you catch more flies with honey.

I kissed him. I plastered my mouth against him, I fused my body with his, and he could feel my curves flattening out on him.

And, of course, he responded.

His dick had been a chub, just half hard, but now it was a sproinger. BOING! Out there. Pointing like an arrow.

I reached down and stroked him and, poor, deprived man, his penis started to drool.

I broke the kiss, and asked, "Is my big, strong man horny?"

"Oh, baby…if you only knew." His eyes were glazed, his breath was hot, his chest was heaving.

"Oh, I do." I patted his cheek and walked into the bedroom.

"Hey!" He followed me in like a well trained dog.

I began taking off my clothes.

He sat on the bed and smiled.

"Unfortunately for you," I said, as I hung up my skirt, "I am totally and utterly beat. Maybe tomorrow."

His mouth opened, his eyes blinked, "But…I've been waiting?"

"Me too, lover." I hopped into bed. "Turn out the lights."

He stood for a second. I ignored him, rolled on my side, scrunched the pillow, and closed my eyes.

Finally, he turned off the lights and slipped onto his side.

And put his arms around me. I could feel his more intelligent half poking me between the buns.

I shifted back and rubbed my buns over his manhood. "Mmm. You've got such a nice dong."

"But…honey, are you really that tired?"

I rolled over and grabbed his erect cock. "Well, I could play with it for a while."

He didn't complain as I stroked his shaft and played with his balls. I kissed him passionately, then said, "And don't cum. I don't want this bed to be a mess."

"I sort of wanted to cum in you."

"That's still a mess. No. Don't cum. Hold it for a while," and I pushed him away and rolled over.

"But…hey!"

"Now, honey," I murmured sleepily, "You don't want me to make love when I don't want to, when I'm this tired. It wouldn't be any fun for me. And you don't want that."

"Well, I…"

Typical man, he didn't care as long as he got his rocks off. Well, my sweet, those days are done. When he pushed up against me this time, with his harder than a rock cock, I pushed him away.

Silly man.

The next day dawned, and I yawned, stretched, and he was all over me. Kissing, slobbering, not even caring about morning mouth.

"Heysoos," I complained in a cheerful manner. "What? Did you stay awake all night?"

"For you I'd stay awake all winter!"

I giggled and pushed him away. I reached down and grabbed my favorite weapon and stroked it. "Doesn't this thing ever run down?"

"Not when you're around."

"Excellent," I said, and I slipped out of his grasp and out of bed.

"Hey!"

I stood next to the bed, hand son my hips, and watched him with a smile, "We've got to talk."

"Oh, fuck." He actually rolled over, faced away from me.

"Well, if you would rather not," I headed for the shower. I like showers.

I barely had the water hot before he slipped into the shower with me. He soaped my body and I soaped his cock.

"Somebody wants to talk, after all."

"Absolutely," he pushed his soapy penis through my hands.

I tried to hold him steady, but he was too well lubricated I finally stopped his surging hips by grabbing his balls.

"Oh, yeah," the breath just whistled out of him.

"Honey," I said. "We're going to have a Female Led Relationship."

"Yeah, sure." His eyes opened. "What's that?"

"I'm in charge."

"What does that mean?"

I stroked his shaft again. "It means that I call the shots. I make the decisions."

"And what do I do?"

"What you're told."

"I don't think I—"

"Do you like this?" I squeezed his shaft for emphasis.

"Uh, oh...yeah."

"Then you'd better do what I say. Now rinse off and get to work."

I stepped out of the shower, and I grinned when I heard him wail in protest.

I was wearing a peignoir, with my half bra and panties, when he entered the kitchen.

I had fixed a good breakfast. Some day I wouldn't, some day he would fix the breakfast, but little steps had to be taken before I had him housebroken.

"Wow," he said, reaching out for me.

"Easy, tiger. Eat up. Sex comes later."

He sat down with a frown, then smiled. Bacon and eggs, waffles with lots of butter and syrup. just the way he liked it.

I sat down opposite him. "Honey, how long have you been working at Rod's Car Shop?"

He shrugged. "Couple of years." He chewed like a caveman, but that was all right with me.

"And you're the best mechanic he has."

"Yep."

"You've reached the point where you can just listen to a car and know what's wrong with it."

He nodded. He was gobbling. He was in hog heaven, literally.

And I thought, *sex and food. And that's all there is.*

Oh, I knew there was more, but right then, watching him abuse his table manners, you can't blame me my thoughts.

"How long have you been talking about starting your own business?"

He stopped chewing and eyed me. "So that's what this is about."

"Yep."

He sighed. "I'm not quite ready, yet."

"And I'm not quite ready to spread my legs and fuck you till your bone near falls off."

His jaw dropped.

I was smiling, had delivered a death knell, and he opened his mouth to—

"Oops, look at the time! You've got to hurry or you'll be late!"

I pushed a bag of lunch into his hands and shoved him towards the door.

He was trying to think of something to say, trying to get on top of the situation, but I had already delivered the coup de grâce.

I opened the door and pushed him out. Sam Randall, our neighbor, was just walking past and he got a full view of my charms.

"Hey!" Randy blurted.

I laughed. "Somebody might as well enjoy me…if you're not going to." I closed the door.

All was silent, and I knew he was just standing there, wanting to come back in, to have it out, to…get his cock roasted.

Then I heard his footsteps down the hall.

Silly man.

Feminizing a man, taking away his manhood by chastity, is a delicate process. It can be done easily by any woman, but the woman has to remember one crucial thing. The man has to want it. And how does he want it? When his cock takes charge and starts making the decisions.

So I had to think things through, read up on the whole procedure, make plans, and that sort of thing.

I couldn't be a bitch, even if I was. I had to be the sexy siren luring him to his...betterment.

And it would be betterment. He would get new goals, achieve new heights, and he would be better. And here's something that a lot of women don't understand, one of the goals of feminism is a man's betterment.

Hey, it's not a matter of who wears the pants, it's a matter of both parties functioning at a higher level.

Anyway, I had a lot of reading to do, and planning, and in addition to the aforesaid matters I had to write 5,000 words, do my marketing and publishing, and keep myself producing.

I didn't make a lot, I was just beginning, but I was on an upward trend. It's just a matter of persistence, educating yourself, and making your own good luck.

So I worked, and I didn't even take time to change my peignoir for clothes. Which was good. It made me feel sexy, and powerful, and that translated into my writing, and even spurred me to go the extra mile when I researched what was needed for a guy to open his own garage.

Five o'clock came before I knew it, and I ran for the bedroom. Randy would be home in 15, and I wanted to be ready for him.

I put on a tummy shaper with straps and rolled my nylons up. I changed my bra for a skimpier one, really held my boobs out. I put on high heels and sat down at my make up table. I worked quick, and when I heard the door opening I was ready.

He stepped into the living room, and I sauntered out of the bedroom, and his eyes popped.

"Holy heysoos with a flat tire on his Rolls Royce!"

"Hello, honey. I missed you." And with that I launched myself at him. Voracious kisses as I tried to suck his tongue right out of his mouth. I dropped to my knees and tried to suck his cock right off his body.

He moaned, was REAL close, and I stood up and said, "Sit down at the table and I'll get dinner."

Dazed, he sat down, and I put ice cubes in a glass, half filled it with bourbon, and half with Coke. It was a 'Coke High,' and he loved them.

"Wow. What's the occasion?" He sipped.

"This," I tossed the business plan on the table.

He looked at the half dozen pages I had typed out...and his eyes rolled. "You expect me to read this? I've had a long day and..." blah, blah, blah.

While he talked I opened the fridge, pulled out a couple of rib eyes, and slapped them in a pan. While they sizzled I sat down across from him and sipped at my own Coke High.

"Honey, I don't actually want you to read that business proposal."

He blinked. "What?"

"I don't want you to do anything you don't want to."

"Well, that's…"

"I wrote that up for me. It's not for you."

"You're going to open a garage?"

"Maybe, but I'll tell you this…"

"What?"

"If you do read that proposal," I leaned towards him, almost close enough for kissing, "I will extract one drop of semen from your cock."

"What? Wait…what?"

"One drop of semen. You give me one drop of semen and I'll let you read my business plan."

Well, let me tell you, he was one flummoxed ox.

He wanted to cum in the worst way. And I was going to let him cum…in the worst way. But his mind was mixing it all up. He saw a drop of sperm as a huge cum. He, with his male mind, didn't really listen to the fine print.

"If I read this…your thing, you'll let me cum."

"One drop." I smiled. He still didn't get it.

"Okay."

So he read, and I dropped a delicious steak in front of him and poured him another drink, and he kept reading, and he frowned and… then he was done.

He stared at the remains of his beef and I asked, "What?"

"Well, that's…"

"Hey, I'm a writer, I do research, but I don't have roots in reality. So what's wrong with the proposal?"

"Well, Rod has a different way of billing vendors. Yours would work, but it's more ideal than real."

"How would you do it then?"

He explained it while I made him another drink and made mental notes for the revision.

"What else?" I asked.

"There's more efficient ways of…" and he continued with a sort of blank-eyed lecture as he took apart my business plan.

And I marveled. Barbara had lectured us on the differences between men and women, and I could see it now. Heck, I had lived with this man for years, and I was only now starting to see him.

Men are strange creatures. They are silly with their obsession with peckers and pussies, but when you can actually get them to focus on something, holy crap! They start throwing distractions to the side, obsess, and march on a straight line.

Great for armies and industry, but…how to get them focused?

And you know the answer. Sex.

Get them to look at work and think sex and you can't stop them.

An hour later he had several sheets of paper out, had fixed my proposal, and suddenly looked up. "You bitch," he said. But it was a flat statement, no animosity. He had been played, and he knew it, but it was for his betterment, so how could he get grumpy?

"Yes, I am. But I'm your bitch."

He stared at me. His one track mind suddenly derailed—heck, he had accomplished his objective, making my theory into a working plan—and he was back on the other track. The sex track.

"Let's fuck."

"I've got a better idea."

"What?" He was breathing hard, ready for his reward.

"Come with me."

I grabbed him by his handle and manhandled him into the bedroom. He was on his tip toes, harder than a crow bar and ready to pry my legs apart. But I wasn't having any of that.

"Lay down."

I got on the bed, on his back. His manhood pointed towards the high ceiling.

I knelt next to him and took a hold of his cock. I stroked it, felt the veins throbbing. With my other hand I gripped his balls.

"Oh, God," he blurted.

"Been a while, eh?"

"Forever."

Which made me giggle. It had only been a couple of days. But, then, men are inexhaustible. Right?

I stroked him quietly. He reached for my breasts and I moved so he could access them. I managed to keep stroking, and enjoyed the feel of his fingers on my nipples.

"Oh, man," he breathed.

I eased off. "Too close, tiger. We have to make this last."

"You make it last, I need to get off."

"Spoken like a true idiot," I grinned.

He laughed, and groaned. "Oh, fuck."

He backed away from the big O and I resumed stroking.

"Do you remember when I said we were going to have a female led relationship?"

I could feel a bit of back off in him. He wanted to cum.

"That means I'm in charge of everything, and especially your sex."

He was silent.

"Do you like this?"

"Yes," with tons of unsaid thoughts.

"Do you like when I play with you like this?"

No brainer. "Yes."

"Well, this is a female led relationship. This is what happens when you give up control of your sex to me. Do you like it?"

He gulped. "Yes."

He was close, so I backed off.

"Hey?" But it was weak. He knew I wasn't going to leave him high and dry.

"I'm not going to make you open a shop." I resumed stroking. "But if you want to look at it, just look at it, that would be great. It's not going to hurt to look at the idea, right?"

"Yeah, but I'm not ready."

I smiled and kept working. The shiny, slick skin of his cock felt wonderful in my hands, and I knew he was on the total edge.

"Then you're not ready. But when you are ready you'll really be ready."

"But what if I'm never ready?"

"Then you aren't. Are you close?" I knew he was.

"Oh, yeah!" he thought I was going to shoot him off.

I let go. His cock throbbed and pulsed and ripped.

He stared at me.

I waited.

I began stroking again.

"Oh...uh..." he was right on the edge, and I slowed down, squeezed hard so he wouldn't suddenly erupt.

"Have I told you would a studly fellow you are?"

Now he couldn't talk.

"I know I was mean the other night, but I know you work hard. I just want to help you."

Nothing he could say to that. His hips started to rise up and I backed off. No way I was going to let him take control of this cum.

"I love you because you're a manly man and you let me do this to you. You are letting me do this, aren't you?"

"Oh...oh...yeah." Now he was having a hard time gulping. His whole body was quivering with desire.

At that point there was so much I wanted to do. I wanted to shape him to my way of thinking, start the feminization, but I had to stop, regroup, take my time.

One does not build Rome in a day.

So I kept stroking, and he kept edging closer and closer, and finally it was too much, I knew he was going to cum.

I stopped stroking. I held him, and I felt the pulse in his cock. I felt his ball sac contract, I felt the semen moving up the shaft, and I squeezed.

"AH...ARGH...AH..."

One drop.

"LET GO! LET GO!"

One, shining drop oozing out of his slit, then no more.

He tried to pry my hands off, but I ignored him. I watched his face contort, turn red. I felt his body lurching, trying to squeeze more out.

No good. I had him under control.

After a minute the surges lessened.

He sank back on the bed.

I ran my finger over his slit and scooped up the semen. I held it in front of him.

"One drop," I said. "As promised." I tasted my finger and he stared at me.

Then I lay down on him, hugged him, and we were lost in our own thoughts.

My thoughts were plans and manipulations.

His thoughts were…blasted.

He couldn't think. He didn't understand what had happened. He wanted more, but he knew it was done.

PART TWO

"Oh, man. I'm horny."

He reached for me, but I was already rolling out of bed.

"Hey!"

"Time for work, my big man."

And he was big. Real big. The 'extraction' had only made him. hornier. He still had a full load, and his libido was totally jacked up.

I hopped in the shower and he was behind me. Literally behind me, his cock poking into my buns.

"Soap me," I said, handing handing him the loofah.

Well, he lathered me up in fine style. He scrubbed my boobs, cleaned my snatch, poked a finger in me, and I was breathing hard, but, baby, I was clean.

I stepped out and, again, he was right behind me. I held out my arms, "Dry me."

He grabbed a towel and near buffed the skin off my body.

I giggled. I liked being in charge.

I turned and dried off his cock.

Lord, it was already leaking pre-cum.

"Baby, we got to do something about this," he kissed my neck.

"And we will, later."

"But I need to get rid of this before work. I need..." blah, blah, blah.

I turned him and pushed him, naked, out of the bedroom. "Go make breakfast."

For a second I thought he wasn't, but he was coming along fine. Barbara had said that men adapt remarkably well, and she was right. He trotted down the hall, pecker bouncing, and I heard him rattling around in the kitchen.

I put on a flimsy negligee, high heels and make up. Eventually I would remain fully clad, work on his imagination, but in the early stages I had to let him see what he was working for.

I sauntered into the kitchen, swinging a pair of my thongs on one finger.

He was mid mix everything, but he turned and stared. His mouth opened at the sight of my jutting breasts. His tongue rolled out like a red carpet at how my nipples were erect. I slapped him in the face with a toss of the thong.

"What's this?" He frowned.

"An experiment," I said.

"What kind of experiment?"

"I'm researching a type of character. I need to know how a man reacts to wearing a thong."

"Well, use your imagination." He held the thong out to me.

I ignored the thong and grabbed a piece of toast out of the toaster. I sat down and started buttering it. Lots of butter, lots of jelly. "Imagination works best when you root it in reality. I need you to wear those all day, and tell me how it felt."

"I can't do that!"

"Why not?" I looked at him levelly. "I help you with a business proposal, the least you can do is help me with a writing concept."

"I can't wear...these!" He held them up like he was afraid to really touch them. "They're women's underwear."

"Men wear thongs."

"Yeah, but I don't, and these are women's thongs."

"I knew it." I smiled triumphantly.

"What? What did you know?"

"I knew your manhood would be threatened."

"My manhood isn't threatened."

"Look at the way you're acting right now. A little piece of material is terrifying you. It's like you think that if you put those panties on your cock is going to fall off."

Now the funny thing is that while we were talking his pecker was bouncing like a ten year old on a trampoline. It was dripping. I almost mentioned that, but I felt like it would be too soon. His bobbing cock was more of an indication at this point. I didn't want to scare the poor sap off.

"My cock is not going to fall off if I put these panties on."

"Then do it. Prove it. Prove that you're a man."

He frowned. He couldn't quite figure out how putting on women's underwear was going to make him a man.

I reached over and grabbed his cock. I spoke to it. "Is hims afraid of a little pair of panties?"

"Cut it out," but he wasn't moving away. In fact, his knees were shivering a bit.

I took the piece of toast I had buttered and jellied and held it up.

"Is hims hungry?"

I shook his penis so it went up and down like it was nodding.

"Hey..."

I wrapped the toast around his dick and started stroking.

"Oh, fuck!"

Butter and jelly and crumbs dripped all over the place.

"Oh, fuck," he repeated, but his tone of voice was becoming desperate.

I stroked him for a while. I stood up and kissed him, but I didn't let him hug me. I didn't want to mess up my negligee. I did let him feel my boobs. And, man, did he feel.

I pushed him away. "Go clean yourself up. I'll finish the breakfast."

He turned and walked out of the room, he moved like a wind up doll.

"And if you don't have that thong on I will be very upset."

He stopped at the door and turned. He was conflicted. He wanted to clean up, to follow my instructions, but he also wanted to leap on me and have his way.

"How upset?" he asked, his throat sounding like a frog was in it.

I held up a finger. "One drop upset." I smiled.

He grinned. He was sweating, messy, ready for another shower, but he was grinning. He liked this game. He turned and headed for the bathroom.

I quickly cleaned the mess on the floor and finished the breakfast. I had everything on the table when he came back in. He was wearing the thong.

I smiled. On one hand, he was uncomfortable, his balls hung out the sides, and I was sure his little, brown button was getting massaged. On the other hand, he was horny, and he had done what I had said.

I smiled. "Oh, baby. That's sexy."

His face was red. "It is?"

"You're making me hot. If you didn't have to go to work I'd jump your bone."

"You would," he sure looked interested in that, and it was overcoming his sense of humiliation.

"Oh, yeah. My research said this thing of men wearing women's underwear was sexy, but...wow!"

He preened.

"Now sit down and eat. You're going to be late."

He sat, and suddenly he wasn't shivering like a little boy. In fact, he was almost proud. Proud of his little thong panties. I almost giggled, it was so cute.

And I realized something. Barbara had hinted at this, and with a big smile, but the reality, woosh. Exerting power over my man was sexy. It was warming. It...made me wet.

Well, good news for me, I had a vibrator, and as soon as Randy went off to fight the dragon I would be hiding in my cave and doing nasty things to my body.

So Randy went off to work, to bust his butt, and to be kinky and horny because of the unfamiliar and even uncomfortable thong he was wearing.

An hour later I called him. I timed it for his break, so he had the time.

"Honey?"

"Yes?"

"Baby?"

"Are you all right?"

"I need you."

He was silent.

"You made me so horny this morning, and seeing you in those panties, well, it almost made me cum on the spot."

"Really," he blurted. I could see him in my mind, suddenly proud and pushing his chest out.

"Really. In fact, you know what I'm doing? Right now?"

"What?"

"I'm feeling my breasts. My boobs. I'm...oh, my God! That feels good."

"Uh..."

He would be standing slack jawed now.

"I'm reaching down to my pussy now. Oh, fuck. It's wet. It's really wet. You've made me so wet."

"Uh...yeah."

Hah! That catch in his voice. Somebody was standing near him and he didn't want them to know he was getting off on dirty, little phone sex.

"My finger is inside me now."

"Oh, fuck," he breathed.

"You're in my panties, right now. How does it feel to be in my panties?"

"Good. It feels...good." He was breathing hard. No doubt his boner was pushing out at his work coveralls. He probably had to turn a bit to hide his excitement from the other guys.

"Honey, I know it's bad, but I need to cum."

"Oh..."

"I need to cum bad. You've got me so horny. I can feel your dick in me. Can I cum?"

"Well, yeah." Duh.

"I'm going to, I'm so close, but if I cum now I won't be so horny when you get home."

""Maybe you'd better wait."

"But I can't!" I whined. "I need to cum now! Tell me to cum now! Please, Randy...please! Tell me to cum."

I could feel the wheels going around in his head. He was getting off on this, but...I wouldn't be horny tonight...but he was getting off on this.

"Randy!" I'm a great actress, it sounded like I was almost sobbing, like my life would end if I didn't have an orgasm.

And, tell the truth, this scene was really working on me. Suddenly I felt like I did need to cum!

"Please! Help me! Let me squirt!"

"Okay," he blurted.

I didn't waste time. I was on the edge, and I pushed on over...and was in freefall...high in the sky...a white heat washing through me. "Oh...God! Fuck...fuck..."

It was real, and he knew it was real, and he listened as I eked out every shiver out of my cum.

Finally. "Oh, geez. Thank you, honey. You really know how to satisfy a woman!"

"Ah, yeah."

Hah!

"Now pull up your panties and go to work, my big...BIG, strong man."

I hung up the phone, and smiled, and wiped the sweat off my face. Damn, that had been a good one!

I was going to have to do this again. Maybe for lunch. Could I get off again? I'll bet I could. I mean, this was hot!

Poor Randy. He got home and he was so-o-o...Randy! He was all over me.

I just giggled and pushed him back.

"Easy, honey. I'm all fucked out."

The disappointment on his face was legend. It was like somebody had just told him he had a dread disease.

"Now take your clothes off. I want to see that thong while I fix dinner."

So we wound up in the kitchen, him naked except for his thong, and me, fully clothed, but quite sexy. My breasts stood out under my blouse, and he couldn't take his eyes off them. My hips were round and luscious, and he kept placing a hand on my butt.

I flipped my hair back and he moaned.

Imagination. I told you.

"Ow!" I said, and placed a jar back on the counter.

"What?"

"I think I strained my wrist. Let me sit and rub it. Do you mind helping a little?"

Of course he didn't, and shortly he was peeling potatoes and shredding cheese and other manly things.

I nursed my perfectly fine wrist and said, "Maybe I need a little pain reliever."

He looked blank.

I nodded at the bottle of bourbon.

"Oh, yeah," he smiled happily and poured us a couple of drinks.

And there I sat, relaxed and comfy, while my man fixed dinner. And it was easy. It had become easy when I had started acting sexy, and primed his pump, so to speak, and not given him any relief.

Well, one drop, but that wasn't really relief, if you get what I mean.

"What was it like wearing that thong all day?"

"Oh, it was weird."

"But sexy. Was your cock hard?"

"Oh, yeah. But you helped with that."

"Oh?"

"Did you really have an orgasm on the phone?"

"Two," I grinned. "And, I hate to tell you this…"

"Yeah?"

"They were better than…than dick enhanced cums."

"Better than if my dick was in you?"

I tried to look sorrowful, even as I exulted. "Yes."

"Well," he tried to be magnanimous. "I guess that's all right."

"What's worse is we're going to do this again."

"Huh?"

He turned away from the skillet and looked at me.

"I'm going to give you another article of women's clothing to wear under your clothes, and I'm going to call you again. I mean, those cums were really good. Are you going to be mad if I have a few more."

"Well, uh…"

"In fact, I'll give you a choice."

"What choice?"

"Do you want to wear a bra…or nylons?"

"I don't think…" he looked worried.

"God, I can just imagine you. Your hard dick, getting harder all day, and bringing it home to me."

"But you won't want to make love if you've been getting off all day."

"I will! I promise I will. Even if I don't…I'll fuck you. I'll even play act with you."

"Play act?"

"I can dress up like a school girl, or a nurse…or a stripper! I'll pretend to fight you off and you can carry me into the bedroom and have your way with me. Would you like that?"

Oh, God. Role playing was his favorite. All I had to do was say, 'Please, Mr. Randall,' like I was a secretary, and he was all over me.

"Well, I guess…"

"Oh, goodie! Do you want to wear the nylons or the bra?"

Bless Barbara and her horny parents. When they got the gleam in their eyes they had turned out a good one. She was so totally right about men and their responses and how they could be manipulated…the next day I got Randy into BOTH the bra (and panties) and nylons.

Imagine that. Two days, and he was in three articles of female clothing. And he wasn't cumming. And he was happy. And fixing breakfast for me.

Fuck!

I, of course, turned up the heat.

I called him at morning break, lunch and afternoon break. I begged for permission to cum. I rubbed my pussy and I did cum. And it was the most glorious squirt I had ever had in my whole borned days!

And when he got home, his pants entering the apartment before him, by about six inches, I had bad news for him.

"Honey," I put a distraught look on my face.

"What?"

"I started my period!"

I fell into his arms and cried.

He, of course, was disappointed, but understanding.

And I was lying.

Finally, after him soothing me and telling me it was all right, I smiled up at his loving face. "Of course, I can still play with you. Would that be okay?"

"Well…" No brainer. "…yeah."

I grinned. "Good. Take off your clothes and tell me how your day in sexy underwear went.

Oh, I had fun. I acted like a school girl, saying, 'No, Mr. Randall! What would the other teachers say if they knew you were sucking on my tits!'

And: 'Oh, Mr. Randall, you're so bad! You make my pussy so wet!

And, 'Oh, Doctor Randall! I think I have a problem with my pussy. Could you examine my pussy and tell me what's wrong?'

And, of course, I kept pushing him away, and he was thinking that I didn't want him to see that I was on a period.

But the capper of the evening, the sexiest thing we did all evening, was: "I called some vendors."

"What?"

He was laying on the bed, his panties down and my hands working his cock like it was a Maypole.

"I called some vendors. I was just curious. Did you know Goodrich has a special on tires? You can get them for $4.95 a piece. You'd have to buy them twelve at a time."

He sat up. "Five bucks!"

"What?"

"Rod said he has to pay $50 bucks a tire!"

"That's a lot of profit."

I could see the dollar signs rolling around in his skull, ching ching ching. Four tires a hundred bucks a tire to the customer. Four hundred dollars. Cost to him, $20. Ka ching!

"Lay back," I pushed him back and went back to stroking him.

"And batteries are under ten."

Ka ching! He sat up. $150 per batter, $140 profit. Installation was a snap. Give that for free and the customers would line up.

My manicured hand, with my sexy, red nails, pushed him back. Stroke, stroke.

"And belts…do you know how much belts cost?"

Ka ching! Ka ching!

And every time he sat up, his eyes translating sex into dollar signs, I got wetter and wetter.

Man, I was going to be calling him all day long tomorrow, and I wasn't going to be faking.

Disaster, of course, was waiting in the wings.

Three days and he was permanently wearing women's underwear. He looked so cute in his tummy shaper, and I was telling him that he could get away with wearing some falsies under his work coverall. And I was having him wear some falsies around the house.

Three days, and he was going out of his mind. Me calling him all day, me jacking him all night. Not being able to see my perfect body (I was wearing clothes most of the time, and even a robe and pajamas). He was a dripping, waiting to happen mess.

Three days, and he popped into the shower and I knew what he was doing.

I waited, listened outside the bathroom, then stepped in and opened the door.

Oh, man, it was perfect. He was mid squirt. He panicked. Tried to squeeze his own cock, but his semen just kept dribbling out.

I stared at him, terribly disappointed. He stared at me, and mumbled apologies. His face was redder than Rudolph's nose.

Having ruined his orgasm, I walked out to the kitchen and waited.

He came in a couple of minutes later. Wearing a robe.

"Look, I'm sorry, babe. It's just, with you being on the rag, and we're talking every day…"

"So you just run your seed down the drain. But I like playing with you, and you take that away from me."

"You can still play with me."

"Open your robe."

He blinked. He opened the robe. Naked. No panties, no bra. Nothing.

I started crying.

"Honey! I said I'm sorry!"

Well, I carried on, and the big sap fell for it. Finally, through tears I said, "If you want me to forgive you you're going to have to do three things."

"Sure. Anything. just tell me."

I sat back, snuffled, wiped my nose, dried my eyes, and said, "First, I want to spank you."

"What?"

"Admit it. You've been a bad, little boy, and you deserve a spanking."

Well, he didn't real 'deserve' one, but he needed one, and I needed to give him one. It would be further assertion of my power over him.

"Well, I don't…"

I upped the tears. Man, once you get going it's easy to keep crying. Sort of fun, too.

"Okay…okay! What's the second thing?"

"I'm going to get you a chastity belt."

"What?" His voice went up a couple of notches. "I'm not going to…"

"I work and I slave! I fix dinner!" Well, actually he was fixing dinner more than me, but that was a moot point. "I put out for you, I play phone sex and stroke you all night! I let you wear my underwear…and you waste it all down the drain! Like a common masturbator! Just a…a jacker offer!"

"Honey…"

He didn't stand a chance.

I stood up and walked out. Into my bedroom. 'My' bedroom. And slammed the door. And locked it. Oh, I know he heard that click.

We had rarely fought during our marriage, but twice he had got me so mad I had locked him out and made him sleep on the couch.

Now it was three times.

I woke up the next day smiling.

He was out on the couch, sleeping on that lumpy couch, and I took off my clothes and put on my half bra and a negligee and skimpy panties. I made myself up and went out to the living room.

"Honey, I'm sorry I was so mad at you."

Well, he was glad that was over, and, tell the truth, though I enjoyed it, I did enjoy the carrot more than the stick.

"Will you forgive me?"

He looked at my tits.

"I guarantee, when I am over my period I will extract TWO drops from you."

He laughed. I giggled. It was all fun and games again.

"But I am going to buy a chastity tube for you."

He sobered.

"Maybe you won't wear it, but you know I'm right. A man shouldn't be jacking off when he's got a perfectly good pussy at hand."

His voice was low, almost embarrassed, when he said, "But you haven't been letting me fuck you."

"And I probably won't."

He took in his breath.

"Not for a while. This is too much fun. Having you all horny all the time? And, admit it, you're having fun going to work and being horny all day."

"Well, I, uh…"

"Admit it!" I reached over and grabbed his erect cock.

"Okay," he whispered.

And, here's the funny thing, he was so messed he didn't even ask me what the third thing was. That was okay. I sort of wanted it to be a surprise.

I kissed him, leaning over the back of the couch, stroking his cock, and all was right in Whoville.

Six days into my supposed period and the chastity tube arrived. Just in time. Tomorrow or the next day he expected to get a little.

Heck, he expected to get a lot.

I opened the box and spread the pieces out on the kitchen table and stared at them. Rings, spacers, tube, lock. Whew. Who would expect such a nefarious device to be so simple?

Well, I talked extra nasty to him that day. And I really got off. I mean I had the equivalent of supernovas happening in my pussy. And when he got home and saw what was on the kitchen table his eyes bulged, his mouth dropped, but…he was horny.

A couple of days since he had jacked off, and he had had time to recover. I tell ya, men never seem to really empty out.

He stared at the chastity tube.

"Pretty, huh?"

"I wouldn't call it that."

"Would you like to try it on now?"

"Uh, no."

So I left it on the table, pushed it aside for dinner, and when the dishes were done he pulled it out for easy inspection.

And he inspected it.

He stared at it, harder than he stared at me.

He touched it, held the pieces of it up and examined them.

I ignored him. Gave him a couple of Coke Highs, and waited.

Men are curious. Especially when it comes to their cocks.

You look at the internet and it is amazing what men will put their penises in. I have seen instances of men putting their cocks in the water outlet in the sides of swimming pools, in hornet's nests, one guy even rubbed his cock with the belt from some sort of band saw. Mangled the poor thing, but that's men.

Randy wasn't that bad, but he was bad.

Finally, he said, "I guess I could try it on."

"Go ahead." I pretended I didn't really care that much. I really just wanted him to get lost in it. I knew he wouldn't be able to get it on.

"I can't get it on," he said. He stood in the doorway, the tube half on his hard cock.

"Why not?"

"I'm too big!"

Oh, poor boy. The way he said that was so prideful.

I sighed. "So what do you want to do about it?"

"I don't know. Doesn't seem to work so…"

"You could pack your cock in ice."

"I think not!" And the concept really seemed to upset him.

"Well, then…what?"

"We could fuck?" he smiled hopefully.

"You could jack off."

Boy, after my little hissy fit he wasn't willing to do that.

"Well," I said. "I suppose I could extract a single drop of cum."

Now, I hadn't fucked him for ten days. And he had had one ruined jack off session, and that had been a couple of days ago. He was primed. And eager. And even eager for a ruined orgasm.

He wanted sex that badly.

So I took him in the back room, loved him, kissed him, fondled him, and…drip.

And now that he understood the procedure, and was so horny, it was easier than the first time.

I grinned and slapped his ass. "Okay, slick, let's see what chastity looks like on you."

He grinned, somewhat feebly, and returned to the living room.

Zingo bingo, his now temporarily limp cock fit in the tube and he closed the lock.

He stood there in the middle of the living room and stared at his imprisoned manhood. He looked up at me. "What now?"

"We wait. And when your cock wakes up and tries to get hard… that's when the fun starts." I smiled in a lascivious, but quite evil, way.

It didn't take long, we were sitting and watching TV, and suddenly he grunted.

I turned to him. "What?"

"It hurts."

I looked down. His cock was struggling to get hard, pushing out the edges, pulling his balls up tight against the rings. I smiled.

"But it doesn't hurt too much to continue."

"Uh, no. I guess not." He was moving around and adjusting his package.

I spun over on him. Planted my bare pussy on him and ground down. I kissed him like he had never been kissed in his life.

When we broke he whined, "Oh, heysoos! I don't think I can stand this."

"Nonsense. You're my big, strong man. You can stand anything!"

I kissed him some more. His cock tried harder to bust the plastic.

"Now suck my breasts!"

He was out of control. He wanted so badly, but his only outlet was to...please me!

He bent his head and went to work, and I tell ya, all of his massive sexual energies were redirected into one goal: please me.

He kissed me, he ate me, he massaged my whole body.

He used his mouth and his fingers and plumbed my depths. Finally, I began to quake and shiver. I was gulping and gasping, and he couldn't stop himself. He kept jamming his fingers in me, sucking on my tits, and the ocean rose up and overwhelmed me. A tsunami of sex washed through me. I was lost, high in the clouds as the sun burst inside me.

He wanted to keep going, but I stopped him.

"No! No more!"

He was disappointed, but the edges of his cock pain were gone. He was accepting his fate.

The next few days were absolutely incredible. In locking him up I had released his energy. He wanted to eat me all night, he wanted to work all day. He got nervous if he didn't have something to do, and he could never relax. He...had...to...keep...going!

All of that incredible, infinite and never ending sexual energy was being transmuted into...living. He didn't have to be asked to fix dinner, he just fixed it, and even started cooking better than I did.

And he did the laundry.

And I actually caught him washing windows. Late at night. Couldn't see for shit through them this time of night, but he was spraying them with windex and scrubbing away.

I couldn't believe it. I had unleashed a monster! I had created the Eveready rabbit, after jamming him full of steroids!

And I kept cumming and cumming and cumming.

A couple of weeks into it I called him into the living room.

"Yes, dear?" He was instantly there, ready to serve.

"Look at this."

He sat, looked at the newspaper and was focused. Like a laser. Like a super laser.

"Wow. Look at the rent. We'd have to eat beans for a month."

"I can put fliers out. Thousands of fliers every day. You'll have business by the end of the first week. Give me two weeks and you'll be able to hire somebody."

Now he was doing that fabulous thing men can do, and he even so much better than women. He was focused. Like a man going to war. All his sexual energies were devoted to the problem at hand. His eyes took on a glazed look.

"You've got that list of vendors, I can talk to Bob down at the bank."

He thought some more and I waited.

"Joe said he would let me use some of his tools. I'll need a car jack to start. If I…"

His mind was working faster than Madonna jills off. And I could see it when it happened.

Ka-ching!

Facts and figures. Dollar signs. spinning around like a mirror ball. He was almost giving out light. Profit, loss, special deals, adding up the figures.

He turned to me, "We can do it."

"Yes, we can. But there's something we need to do first."

He waited. He was so damned focused that he was actually patient!

"You never asked what the third thing I wanted was."

But he hadn't forgotten. I could see it in his eyes.

"What is the third thing?"

I stood up and undid my pants. I had worn loose pants anticipating this, and when I dropped them my cock sprung up.

"Holy fuck!" He was on his feet, staring at my groin.

"In a female led relationship there is true equality."

He stared at my strap on cock.

"It's time for you to experience that equality."

"You want to…to use that on…me?" His eyes were shining.

"Yep."

That was a moment. I will always remember the look in his eyes, the way he was breathing, how he started gulping.

But all men are curious. All men think these thoughts. Not all men have the courage to go forward.

"You're already wearing women's underwear, and you're going to wear more. I'm going to make you into my little bitch."

I was smiling quite disarmingly. I wanted him to like the idea, not run screaming into the night.

"It's awful big."

"No. But it's not awful small, either. It's man-sized…it's designed for a real man."

"So I take it up the butt and you'll back me on this owning my own business thing."

"Yep."

I would back him up anyway. But…this was the piece de resistance. This was the icing on the cake. This was the final step in making my man over.

He let out along, trembling breath. "Okay. How do we do this?"

"First, I give you a spanking, then I fuck you."

He blinked. By being deliberately rude about it I was turning him on.

"Where?"

"I'm going to spank you in the living room, then I'll fuck you in the bedroom."

"Okay." His eyes were so shiny. They were inscrutable, looked like they were about to shed tears. But he was willing.

I took him into the living room and laid him over the end of the couch. That wonderful, lumpy couch.

"I'd ask you to be gentle, but that's not the point, is it?"

"I'll be gentle later, when you need it. Right now you need rough."

"Okay."

I went into the bedroom and pulled his belt out of the loops, I returned to the living room and slapped the belt against my hand.

CRACK!

That was the moment he had second thoughts, hearing the sound of that leather on my palm, but I didn't give him a chance to think about it.

WISS…CRACK!

Oh, he jumped, and he started to move his hands back to cover his ass. I pushed his hands aside and: WISS…CRACK!

"Oh, God!" He buried his face in the cushions.

WISS…CRACK!

WISS…CRACK!

I spanked him long and hard. When I was done his butt was a bright red. Far redder than if he had been simply embarrassed.

And he was crying. Tears had come about the tenth stroke, and he had cried until twenty, and then I helped him up.

He was sobbing, and he leaned on me. He cried on me, and the tears felt so good on my skin.

They felt good for him, too. It was cathartic.

I placed him on the bed and started slathering the lube into him.

He jerked under the feel of my hands on his butt, but he managed to hold still while I made sure he was slicker than slick.

Then I stepped between his legs and touched the tip of my dildo to his brown star.

He jerked, and every homophobic thought he had ever had rose up in his mind.

I pushed forward and the head popped into his rectum.

"Oh! Oh!"

Still, he stayed on all fours, quivering and shaking and crying.

I pushed forward and slithered into him.

For a long moment he held it still, then, as if by magic, he started to push back. All his delicate nerve endings were telling him that this was good, that he needed this.

"Oh, God!" He mumbled.

I reached under and gripped his caged cock. And I thought: what a night. Caged, wearing women's underwear, spanked, and now this.

I had far exceeded Barbara's predictions on how fast you can bring a man to total compliance and enlightenment.

"I think I'm going to pee."

"That's fine, honey," I cooed. "You let it happen."

And he did. I had pressed on his prostate and that had forced the semen up the shaft. His cock began to drool sperm.

"Oh, yeah," he said. Relief was heavy in his voice.

For another minute I screwed him, and he screwed back, then I pulled out.

"Oh, God," he murmured, now just sprawled out and laying face down. "I want more."

"And I'll give you more. I'll give you all you want. But first, you need to satisfy me."

Silly man, never running out of sex. I lay down and pushed him and he rolled over. Soon he was face deep in me, satisfying me, using his tongue the way it was meant to be used.

And I thought:

Woman...queen of her castle. And I was going to get a castle.

Man...a force of nature that merely had to be tamed.

And: female led relationship...chastity...feminization...spanking...strap on.

All the factors to make a perfect marriage, if you have the will to make it happen.

END

Full Length Books from Gropper Press

Rick Boston and his beautiful wife, Jamey, move to Stepforth Valley, where Rick is offered a job at a high tech cosmetics company. The House of Chimera is planning on releasing a male cosmetics line, and Rick is their first test subject. Now Rick is changing. The House of Chimera has a deep, dark secret, and Rick is just one more step on the path to world domination!

The Stepforth Husband

The Feminization of Jack

It felt good to be soft

PART ONE

"Oh, no!"

"What?" Molly, my wife looked out of her closet at me.

We were getting ready for a charity auction and I was looking down at my belly.

"Look!"

My belly was protruding, I couldn't get the buttons buttoned.

"Oh, Jack," she laughed. "Did you get preggers?"

"Not funny."

"Well, just suck it up." She started giggling. What a hilarious wife, eh?

"I'm not going."

"Oh, yes. You are. And that is that."

"Well, that may be that, but this is this, and I'm not going. Tomorrow I'll start a weight loss program. Sign up for Weight Watchers, or something."

"Jack," I could almost hear her frowning in the closet. "You know I look forward to these events. They are a lot of work, and they really change lives."

I sighed and sat on the bed. "Well, you'll just have to do without. No way I am going to go looking like a fat slob." I punched my belly roll and wondered how I had gotten in this shape.

Suddenly something hit me in the face.

"Ack...what?"

I held up the item that had been thrown at me. It was a corset.

"Put that on."

"You've got to be kidding!"

"I am not. You are not going to deprive me of my night out, especially after the months of work I've been doing.

"There is no way I can get this on, even if I was willing, which I am not."

Molly came all the way out of the closet then, and she came with an angry lioness look on her face. She stomped towards me, grabbed my shirt with both hands and snarled in my face. "You will go."

Now, my wife is beautiful. She's willowy with boobs big enough to be called mountains, and she works out daily so she is strong. Her face is patrician, with a Roman nose, slender and aquiline. She is...we both looked down.

My cock had sprung up and poked her in the thigh.

We looked at each other. She laughed. "Well, I guess we know who's calling the shots."

"Just because I've got an erection it doesn't mean you can push me around!" Was my voice sounding just a little bit whiney?

"Oh, yes it does. It does!" She reached down and grabbed Mr. Happy and throttled him gently. Her voice changed pitch, became softer, instead of a lion she was now a pussy cat. Her other hand grabbed my testicles. "Honey, you like it when I talk tough to you, and you like it when I talk softly, like now."

"Urk," I gulped.

She lifted, and I went to my tip toes. I pushed down on her wrists but she had the leverage. "Now, we can do this the hard way..."

She held my balls in an iron grip and stroked my cock. Hard.

"Or we can do this the easy way."

She pushed me back and I fell back on the bed. She leaped on me and the look on her face was victorious and smirky all at the same time.

"AGH!"

She slipped over me, engulfed me, and I felt the velvet grip of her cunt suddenly strangling Mr. Happy. She placed her hands on my shoulders and pressed her weight on them.

I couldn't move. Not that I wanted to. There's few things I like more than a good fuck. In, there's nothing I like better than a good fuck. And my wife, to be blunt, is a good fuck.

I felt her muscles gripping me as she corkscrewed her hips, and the edge of her pussy turned and twisted.

"Oh, God!" I reached up and grabbed her awesome mounds. Her nipples were excited and felt rough against my palms.

She kissed me, took my lips in her teeth and pulled, sucked my tongue, fused her mouth to mine.

Well, there was no way I was going to last long with that amount of lust perched on me. I started to push my hips up and she stopped moving.

"Hey!"

She sat stride me, impaled, giving a little shiver, and she said, "You will wear that corset!"

"No!"

"Very well, have it your way." She began to quake. She is an easy cummer, always has been, and now she came quick and fast and hard. Almost manlike. No easy climb and gentle fall, but a sheer blast of white hot fever.

"Hey!" I gasped. I tried to move, but she held her weight on me, kept me immobilized. Her head dropped and her hair hung down to my face.

"Let me move! Let me get off!"

She gave a final shudder, then pushed off me. Her grin was

downright evil.

She stood over me, smirking, and said, "There are those that cum to an event in a corset and get to cum, and then there are the other types of fools. No cum. Doomed to live a life of frustration."

I stared up at her. My cock was glistening with her juices. My heart was pounding. I had been on the edge, and now I was deprived.

"Honey, you can't do this."

"If you wear the corset you will look handsome, debonair, nobody will know, and I will fuck your brains out when we get home."

I was breathing hard, my cock was bouncing up and down madly. That's the thing about being deprived, being. teased and denied, it makes you want it more.

"Now, I'm going to the event, and if you were a manly man you'd suck it up and put that corset on. Or you can be a little pussy and not cum for a week. Or maybe a month. Or maybe not until the next time we have an event—what's that? Three months? Or if we skip it, and we might because of COVID, you could be talking about six months. Maybe even a year."

"I'll jack off."

"Now who's the pussy?" she slid that quip into me like a knife into butter.

Funny, she didn't mind getting herself off, but she was particular vicious at the idea of me getting myself off.

She grabbed my cock. "What's it going to be, bub? Paradise or purgatory?"

I managed to squeak out, "Paradise!"

She grinned. "I'd gloat, but it's not ladylilke. Heh heh heh!" she gloated.

So I took off my shirt and stepped into a corset. Man, she loosened it up, but it was still tight. And it was hell just to get it over my bobbing cock.

"Ooh, I like this!" She kept laughing and slapping my weenie.

Finally, I was in, and now the tough part, she began to lace me up.

"God, you really have been scarfing the cookies!" She knelt on my back and pulled the strings. Slowly, slowly, and with much suffering, my waist became, well, not svelte, but better. And the weird thing, my chest swelled.

She stood me up and inspected me, and took note of the way my flesh had been pushed up. "You've got little titties." She placed her hand over my pectoral and cupped my little mound.

"Hey!"

Sproing! My cock hit her thigh.

She looked down. She looked up at me. She grinned. "If I didn't know better I'd say you liked wearing this female undergarment. You actually like having little titties."

"Hey!" but I was weak. I could hardly breath, I was being bullied, I didn't have enough force in my voice.

She grabbed my handle then and stroked it, and kissed me some more. Then she moved back an inch and spoke into my face. "We're going to have to explore this. Some panties. Maybe a bra." My cock surged and she grinned harder. "The peeny never lies."

"Stop it!" I said. Again, I didn't sound strong.

"Some nylons, and...I've got it, long red nails..." my cock gave a mighty surge... "to go with your bright, red lipstick."

Splurt! I came.

We looked down in shock. My jizm was squirting all over her hand. A lot of white coated her knuckles, dripped on the floor. My knees were weak and shaking.

"Crap," I said. "You jacked me off!"

"Jacked off, hell! You jacked yourself off...with your dirty, little mind."

"Well, now I don't have to go."

Well, she had a hold of Mr. Limpit and she lifted and snarled, "Don't mess with me, cupcake!"

Damned if I didn't have an aftershock. Not a cum, not more sperm, but a shiver that went through me, weakened my knees, unfocused my eyes.

"Holy crap!" Molly muttered. Awestruck. "Holy...holy, crap!"

We went to the event. I was in the corset already, and you couldn't see it, and, let's face it, she had a hold of my prized possession, and she threatened to rip it off.

But underneath everything I could feel this lust in her. This excitement. This drive to control and hold sway over me.

She liked having this power over me.

All night long the knowledge was in her eyes. She smirked at me, dropped sly little hints that were sexy, funny innuendos to those around us, but bombshells to my addled state.

I had, after all, cum. And just from putting on a corset. And hearing all those things she said, about putting me in a bra, making me wear make up.

And, when we danced, she tried to take control. And she even put her hand on my chest, a simply placement that was understandable between husband and wife, but electrifying to my scrunched up boob.

Was this what women felt when a man played with her breasts? Did they get that shiver of excitement from a man squeezing them? And when her palm slid across my nipple I thought I was going to swoon.

She took note of my reactions and just laughed. And did them some more.

Driving home we had a conversation. It was one of the more impactful conversations in my life.

"I'm going to feminize you a little."

"I don't think so."

"But you so obviously love it. Did you feel how hard your dick was? And you came when I talked about putting you in lipstick."

"I did not!"

"Did!"

"I was just super horny. I'd been in you, you came and I didn't. I was so fucking horny I would have exploded if…if Hillary Clinton waved her ass at me."

"Lotta ass, lotta cum," quipped Molly.

"So, no. That's it. No."

"Head over to Charley Coyote's."

"What?"

"I want a drink."

"We can have one at home."

She turned to me, leaned across the center console and touched my nipple. I shivered. "Just one, widdle, bitty dwink?"

She knows I hate baby talk. Nothing irritates me like baby talk.

"Pwease?"

"Oh, fuck. Okay."

"Excellent."

I took a turn and headed for the most popular nightspot in town, at least popular for those in the know.

We didn't say anything for a minute, then she started chuckling.

"What?"

"You are so fucking easy."

I snorted, then grinned. She was right. But wouldn't you be easy if a super sexy woman was stroking your gonads?

We pulled into the parking lot and an attendant stole my car. We walked around to the front and through the entrance. This was a Thursday, and it wasn't frantic. Just crazy. A low mumble of people, a combo on the stage whispering dirty sax songs, and the heady smell of sex.

We sauntered in and looked around. "I'll grab that table. You get me something sweet that turns me on."

I headed for the bar, and fortunately I knew the bar guys, and I was a tipper. Jose saw me coming and had my obligatory Coke High ready.

A Coke High. A fancy name for bourbon and Coke. With the good bourbon, of course.

"Something fizzy and fruity for my wife?"

"We have just thee thing." He spoke with a Mexican accent and I laughed.

"Thee? Are you practicing to swim back across the river?"

Jose was born and bred in East LA. He grinned. "Naw. Boss said I'd get more tips if I sounded like a real wetback."

We laughed and he plopped a tall, thin glass in front of me. It was pink with bubbles fizzing up like an Alka Seltzer.

"What is it?"

"Jose's surprise."

I lifted my eyebrows.

"It's called a Pink Squirrel. Creme de noyaux, creme de cacao, and cream."

"Sounds creamy."

"Give her two and you'll get lucky."

We laughed, I dropped him a twenty and said, "For you. We'll run a tab."

"I'm your bitch."

I grinned at him and walked the drinks back to where Molly was waiting for me. And I thought, 'I'm your bitch.' A simple phrase, just a Hollywood expression, but…it made me think. It made me think because I was wearing a corset and Molly had been messing with my head. Panties. Bra. Lipstick.

Long, red, bright, sexy, shiny nails.

Fuck.

I reached our table, it was a booth back in a corner, and placed the drinks down.

"Ooh, what did you get me."

"Jose's Surprise." I struggled into the booth, that damned corset made motion difficult. How did women stand the things?

She looked askance at me, with raised eyebrows over the lip of her glass, as she took a sip.

"He spermed in it."

She almost lost it. She almost spit a bit of that precious liquid out, but she managed to hold it in. A bit of choking, and a cough, but she was good.

She looked over at the bar and raised her hand.

Jose saw her and she gave him a thumbs up. Jose waved and grinned.

She sipped again and faced me. "It was your sperm, if any, but I know you just came. You're empty. Drained. So what is this delicious concoction?"

"A pink squirrel," and I explained the ingredients.

"Crap," she said, "It's better than if he did cum in it."

"You're such a potty mouth," I teased.

Then she went to work on me. I sipped my bourbon and Coke and listened, and she whispered into my ear.

"I can see you all svelte and trim...with big boobs."

I looked at her. She grabbed my chin and turned my ear back to her.

"Big boobs, and wearing a bikini. But the top is too small, it keeps slipping down. Suddenly it falls all the way off. Everybody is staring at you."

"Where are we?" I asked.

"We're at a fancy party, nothing but sexy celebrities. In fact, they're all porn stars, and they all have huge boobs. But nothing like yours. They see your exposed tits and they are all jealous. They all wish they could have your boobs. Then, we're sitting there, and a producer comes over to you. He looks at your huge boobs and wants you to be in his latest flick. The name of the flick is 'He had Woman Boobs and Knew how to Use Them!'"

"I do?"

"Shut up," she pulled my face around and put her mouth so close to my ear I could feel her warm breath. Her moving lips touched my ear, teased it.

"Later, I want to go home, but you're too drunk to drive. So I take you into a bedroom and leave you. When I'm gone three porn stars sneak into the bedroom. They have ben stalking you for your tits. They are so jealous. They want to feel them, they want to suck them. And your cock. they want to suck your cock."

Oddly, the talk of them sucking my tits was more turning on than the idea of them sucking my cock. And that would have bothered me, except that Jose's Cock High...uh, Coke High...was really working.

"The three porn stars only have skimpy, little bikinis on, and they strip them off and cuddle up to you. You wake up, but you are too drunk to move, and they begin to have their way with you. Two of them are feeling your tits. Sucking on your nipples. The third one is sucking on your cock. then you feel one of their hands, you don't know which one, grabbing your butt. She grabs it and feels it and her fingers slide into your crack. You like it. You always wondered what it would feel like to have a pussy, and the way this women is feeling your rectum, you start to understand. Then she slides a finger into you. Then two fingers. You are hot. You feel like you're going to explode. Your cock is getting a mouth job, and she is feeling your nuts, but it's the two mouths sucking on your big tits that is getting to you. You arch, you poke your butt back, she has three fingers in you, and just when you think you are about to cum..."

I was breathing hard. Jose had sent another couple of drinks over and I had sucked half of mine without even being aware of it.

"Just when you are about to cum...you hear me screaming."

I tried to move away, to look at her. This wasn't the way one of her stories was supposed to go. But she held my head firmly and kept breathing into my ear.

"I'm screaming in ecstasy, while you were unconscious I was out in the big room, and you know who was there? Jose. And he had a pink drink, a squirrel thing, and I thanked him for it by getting on my knees and gobbling him. Then he pushed me back, down on my back, and everybody watched while he mounted me. He had a big, huge, Mexican dick. Far bigger than your tiny weenie. Bigger even than all the dicks I had before I was married. So I'm screaming because my hole is getting reamed and it feels so…so…so…how you doing?"

"Fuck!" I whimpered.

Molly's throat rattled with laughter. "We're going to have so much fun."

I just shook my head and sipped my Coke High. And when I was done another one appeared. Now, I don't know, but I think the way that corset was squeezing me was ambushing my ability to intake liquor. I was light-headed from my whole body being choked, and she kept pouring booze into me, and it wasn't long before I knew I wasn't driving home.

"Don't worry about it," Molly grinned. "I'll take care of you."

I was sloshed. "That's what I'm worried about."

"And you should be. Now, drink up, bitch boy."

"What?" But I drank, and the drinks kept coming, and she kept whispering dirty things to me, and telling me how she was going to feminize me, and asking why my dick was so hard when she talked tough to me and told me how she was going to give me nails and lips and dress me up like a Barby, and the next thing you know, I…

…woke up. Oh, fuck. Double fuck. My head felt like it had been drop kicked for a goal. My belly felt like a broken washing machine, spinning around, ka chunk, ka chunk, and the door flies open and I…

…ran for the bathroom. Staggering and slipping and I was caught in something, something was tripping me, and I banged against the bathroom door and just managed to upchuck on the throne. Not in it, unfortunately, but on it, because some fool had left the lid down.

Ra-a-alph! Ra-a-alph! I spewed, splashing the place up, then figuring out what was happening and lifting the lid. Ra-a-alph!

From somewhere far away I heard Molly going 'Ew! Heysoos! In the toilet!"

…awoke. Hurting. My belly aching. My throat tasting like a frog had taken a dump in it. My head…oh, God, my head…

…awoke. And was awake. Stayed awake. Lived with the feeling of somebody tap dancing in my belly. Endured the crash of timpanis in my head. Opened my eyes.

It was noonish, according to the splash of sunlight coming in through the drapes.

I just laid there, pretending that a truck hadn't rolled over my belly and squashed my contents out all over the place. I remembered upchucking. A lot. Fortunately, the pain was more of a memory.

Finally, I rolled over, stuck my feet out, and got out of bed. I swayed. I looked down. I was naked. No damned corset. And I had a weird memory of wearing one of Molly's robes, one of those peignoir things. But I wasn't wearing one now, so it must have been a dream.

I pulled on a robe, my old, tattered one, and headed for the kitchen. Not to eat, that was where we kept the aspirin.

Molly was at the sink, sipping coffee and looking out the window. She turned when I entered the kitchen and smiled. And smiled a lot. Goofy bitch.

"Hey, baby. How you feeling?"

"Gar," I muttered. I made it to the cabinet with the medicines in it and grabbed a couple of aspirin. I tossed them down the gullet and stuck my head under the faucet. After swallowing I left my head there, just let the water run over my head. Cool water.

I straightened up.

"That good, eh?"

I faced Molly. "You let me drink that much. You bitch."

"Hey, I'm not your mother. Or am I?"

"What?"

"Nothing." She was staring at me, and she was—I could feel it—belly laughing on the inside.

"I fail to see the humor in your husband dying."

"It's not that. It's..." she snickered and waved a hand and looked down. Then she looked up, holding a smile in. "Can I get you something? A piece of bread? Hair of the dog?"

"Oh...yeah. I suppose."

She made me a Bloody Mary and I downed it, and immediately my stomach started settling.

"Okay now?"

"Better." I belched.

"Cute. Well, come on. You barfed on my clothes last night, you get to help me hang them up. I already washed them."

"I barfed, eh?"

"Tossed out your kidney and your liver, almost your gall bladder."

"Har dee har..."

She took my hand and led me to the garage. She had me hold the basket and she pulled articles of clothing out of the washer. The corset. The peignoir. A bra. Panties.

"Crap. I really got you, didn't I?"

"No worry," she was smirking. What the fuck was so funny?

Then I had a strange memory. She wasn't there, she was back in bed, or so I assumed. And I was in the bathroom, alone, heaving all over the place. So how had I heaved on her peignoir if she wasn't there?

Confused, I just stood there, well, leaned there, against the machine, and she put her dainty underthings and stuff in it, then she pointed me towards the backyard.

I managed to walk on a sort of a line out to the clothesline. I put the basket down and started hanging things up. Pulled stuff out, shook them to get rid of some of the wrinkles, then pinned them.

I wasn't more than half done when I heard the side gate bang.

"Hey, Jack!"

I pulled my robe tight and tied the sash.

It was Tom and Jenny Hawkins. My neighbors. And a bit more. We had spent a few nights drinking crazy, and one night Jenny had sat on my lap and kissed the hell out of me, while Molly sampled Tom. Nothing but fun.

"Hi, guys. What brings you out here at the crack of dawn."

They sauntered across the lawn to me, and they were staring at me in a weird manner.

"Crack of dawn. Hmmph." Jack stifled a guffaw. My 'crack of dawn' in the middle of noon wasn't that funny.

"Had a bit too much to drink last night?" Jenny put a hand on my arm and her whole face was writhing with merriment.

"Molly told you, eh?"

What the heck was so funny?

"She said you, ah…(chuckle, chuckle) really tied one on."

"You could say that. But I paid the price."

"I guess you did," snickered Jenny.

I blinked and turned to them, gave them my full attention. "Say, what's the joke?"

They lost it. Tommy actually fell on the ground, held his belly and rolled. Jenny just kept looking at me and cackling like an egg had fallen out of her ass.

"What the fuck?" It was actually a little irritating. I mean, I like humor as much as the next guy. But if something funny was happening they should let me know, let me join in the fun.

"Oh, Jack…Jack," Jenny grabbed Tommy's hand and tried to get him off the ground, all she succeeded in doing was pulling herself down, and they writhed in a puddle, laughing hysterically at I knew not what.

"What the hell is going on?"

"Hey, Jack." I turned. Molly was there, with a big smile on her face. Her belly was actually bouncing a little as she stifled her own laughter.

"You, too? What the fuck is so funny?"

Then all three of them were laying on the ground, laughing. I have never seen anybody laugh so hard in my life.

I stood over them, hands on hips, and for the life of me couldn't figure it out.

Jenny struggled to her feet. "Oh, Jack. I could tell you, but...but..." she looked at Molly and Tom, "you would have had to have been there." Then she was falling down again, and the others were laughing even harder.

I shook my head. I was the only sane person in a village of idiots. I hung up the clothes, and every time it looked like they were going to stop laughing...they started up again. Holding their bellies, slapping their knees, laughing like a hyena on laughing gas at a joke convention.

Numbnuts. That's what they all were. A bunch of numbnuts.

I finished hanging the clothes and walked back into the house.

Numbnuts.

I went into the kitchen. There were a couple of dishes in the sink and I did them, and watched my wife friends through the window.

They were still laughing, but they were sitting, cross legged, and talking, too.

What the hell was going on?

Finished with the dishes I went in and sat down in the living room. I turned on the big screen and caught the tail end of a game. I was sitting, leaning forward, actually thinking about some lunch, when Molly came in.

"Well, are you over it?"

"I guess," but she wasn't. She snuffled down a throaty chuckle.

"You could at least let me in on it."

"I could, I suppose. But when there's a major gotcha in the works one doesn't mess with it. One lets it play out."

"So you're playing a practical joke on me?"

She nodded, and held in her laughter.

"It's funny right now?"

She nodded, her lips clamped together. Then she actually walked out of the room and started laughing.

Now, I wasn't feeling all that chipper, and I was confused, and I followed her down the hallway, into the bedroom.

"Honey, fun is fun, but you really need to let me in on the joke."

Her face was writhing, parts of it wiggling, as she tried not to laugh. She said, "Okay, hmph...um...okay. I'll tell you, but you have to do something for me."

"What?"

"Walk into the backyard naked, put on the peignoir, and come back in."

"That's it?"

"Um hmm." She put her hand on her hip and blinked to keep herself contained.

"Okay. I can do that."

"And you have to do it immediately after I tell you."

"Okay," I shrugged. What was so hard about that. "So what's the joke?"

"Go brush your teeth."

Oh, crap. I had something in my teeth, and they were all laughing at me, looking like a hayseed bumpkin or something.

I rubbed my teeth with a finger, which made Molly spurt out a squeak of hilarity, then walked into the bathroom. I looked down at the sink, was glad she had cleaned the puke off everything, grabbed my toothbrush and the toothpaste, started to squeeze out a dollop, and looked up...up...oh FUCK!

I grabbed my mouth! I actually gave a little yelp.

PART TWO

I stared at myself in the mirror. I had a fat belly and the robe had come open a little bit to expose it. My cock, damned traitor, was springing up. My lips were bright and shiny and...red.

Red. Like a sunburned fire engine. Like the color of a red mustang. Like a tomato that's embarrassed.

My hand now shaking I reached up and touched my lips. It wasn't like lipstick, it was like the color of my skin had actually been changed. And my lips actually felt a little...plumper. Maybe it was just the bright red standing out more, but my lips, now that I wasn't focused on my hangover but on my face, felt bigger. Fatter.

Like a real woman's lips.

"Oh..." I said.

"I didn't use lipstick. I used lipstain." Molly was leaning against the door jamb, her lips trembling with laughter. "Good lipstain. Guaranteed for a week. A couple of days from now they'll get a little faded, but we can use a bit of gloss and they'll pop right up."

I turned to her, aghast, my eyes wide. "I can't...you...I..."

"Now go put on your peignoir. And give me that robe. No male clothes for a week."

"But...I...work..."

"I talked to Tom at the event and told him you wanted to take a week off. And, buddy, this week is mine."

"But...but..."

"So give me that robe..." she stepped forward and grabbed my robe and started working it off me. "...and go out in the back yard, naked, like you promised, and put on that peignoir."

"I don't...you can't..."

She pushed me down the hallway.

To tell the truth, I would have welched. I wouldn't have gone out in the back yard, even though Tom and Jenny had already seen me, except that Tom and Jenny were already in the house. About the time we reached the kitchen I was starting to dig in my heels, and they were sitting at the kitchen table. Waiting for me.

"Hey, Jack," Jenny smirked.

Oh, God. My skin was flaming. It had to be the color of my lips.

"Good look, Jack," offered Tom. "Very sexy."

And I just sort of gave up. I stumbled past them, headed out the door to the back yard. Not really seeing much, just glimpses of the lawn, the surrounding bushes, the peignoir hanging from the line.

My cock was hard through all this. It had sprung up, I realized, when I had seen my face in the mirror, and it didn't seem to want to go down.

I reached the peignoir and stood, facing it, gasping for breath like I was having a heart attack. And, who knows, maybe I was.

Molly was suddenly standing next to me, and I realized I had been standing there for a while. My mind had gone into overload and literally stopped working. I was like a moose that had been bashed on the head by a wrecking ball.

"Jack?"

I turned my head and gazed at her. Oh, yeah. My wife. I was married. What was happening to me? Oh, yeah. My face. My lips. She had…she had…

"Are you all right?"

I managed to gulp and give a slow nod.

"Then put on the peignoir and let's go inside."

I nodded again. Gulped. Was aware that I had a siren's lips. Was aware of my lips. I reached out and took the peignoir down. It was dry. I must have just been standing there for a long time.

Molly helped me into it. I was like a five year old being helped into his clothes for his first day at school.

She hooked her arm in mine and walked me back to the house.

Inside the house Tom and Jenny had made drinks.

Drinks. That's what I needed. A lot of drinks.

Forgotten was my hangover. Forgotten was my roiling belly and my aching head. I just needed a drink. I picked a glass off the table and drank the whole thing.

They all stared at me. Tom started to say something, but Jenny nudged him and shook her head.

"Let's all have breakfast," announced Molly.

"Uh, yeah," said Tom.

"Okay," Jenny offered brightly.

I just stood there with my hands on the table and my head down. Breathing. My mind slowly, ever so slowly, coming back to life.

I picked up a second drink, I don't know whose it was, but it was bourbon and Coke, and slugged it down.

Again, Tom looked about to speak, but Molly said, "It's okay. He just needs to figure it out."

"Yeah," I said. "Figure it out." I looked up at the three. They were still smiling, but they were a bit nervous. Apparently they hadn't thought through to the reaction I was having.

I wasn't laughing.

I said to Jenny. "Scoot over."

Jenny slid to the side and I moved in next to her. She was dressed, I was in a peignoir, my hard cock visible through the glass table top.

I looked at Tom, who was across from me. "Hi, Tom."

He blinked, I sounded strange, but he said, "Hi, Jack."

"Hi, Jack," I mused. "I've been hijacked. At least my lips have." I grabbed a third drink. It looked like Tom had sipped from it, but I didn't care.

Tears started to come down my cheeks. I put the empty glass down. Yes, I was crying. Then I had my face down on the table and was sobbing.

Molly, Jenny and Tom were very silent now.

I cried for about five minutes. Then I stopped. Oddly, it was like a light switch being clicked. I suddenly just stopped. I looked at my three friends. They had very worried looks on their faces. I said, "Well, it looks like you got me."

I sniffed a couple of times, then looked at Molly. "Waffles. Lots of butter and syrup. I need something sweet."

Molly stood there.

And, the really odd thing, the world was crystal clear to me at that point. Every color was brighter, filled with life. The lines of the objects of the world were so sharp with clarity. I could even see the motes in the air. Life was, in a way, golden.

"Molly?" I asked, my hyper senses kicking into gear.

"Yes. Right away."

Tom tried, "Jack, we're sorry. We were just having a joke..."

I waved my hand. "And it is funny. A year from now I will be laughing hysterically, and I will always remember this massive 'gotcha.' Right now, I'm okay. I'm just coming to grips with everything."

Jenny blurted. "It's Molly's fault."

Molly spun and stared at her friend.

Jenny: "I'm sorry, but I can't...I didn't know this was going to happen like this."

Again, I waved my hand. "It's fine. Molly is the architect. You guys are just the appreciative audience. I get that."

"I'm sorry, Molly. I shouldn't have said that. I'm just..."

"Scared. Worried. Don't want me to hurt."

"Yes."

"It's okay, babe," I said to Molly. "Jenny's fine. She didn't mean anything. Now get my waffles."

Everybody was blinking and awkward, but Molly managed to turn and attend to the waffles. We had a four slot toaster and she loaded it up, put the butter and a big bottle of Aunt Jemima on the table.

Nobody was talking. Everybody was weird. So I said, "So, Tom, how's work."

It was non sequitur. It was the surrealistic moment. It was four people in a lifeboat and somebody says, 'I think I'll paddle with a sieve."

Then we were laughing. All of us. In hysterics. Couldn't stop laughing for the life of me, of any of us. Tom pounded the table so hard I thought it would break. Jenny put her hands on the sides of her face and roared. Molly held herself up with one hand on the counter, her other hand was against her face. And I...I couldn't stop.

None of us could stop.

For long minutes we laughed, and every time we slowed down we would trade a glance, or look at my lips, and start all over again.

Then the toast started burning. A little wisp of smoke rose up and Jenny pointed at it and we found that absurdly hilarious.

And we laughed and laughed and laughed.

I stood in the bathroom and stared at my lips. Red. And the rest of my face was no long as red. It had been a couple of hours, I had eaten and was over my hang over, and even my short spate of breakfast drinking. And I was actually admiring my lips.

They were full, apparently Molly had used plumper on them, long lasting plumper, and they were like a billboard in the desert of my face.

"What do you think?" Molly came and stood next to me, linked an arm in mine, and studied my face in the mirror.

"Major gotcha. Don't think I'll ever top that."

"Probably not, but I was speaking of your mouth. Pretty sexy, eh?"

"I never would have thought," I agreed. I touched them. Lipstain. Long lasting. Wouldn't come off for rubbing. And I knew she was going to keep putting on the plumper. She had 'freshened me up' with the plumper once already.

"And we're going to do the whole you."

"The whole me. Wow."

I looked at myself and not her. But then, right at that moment I was the more fascinating of us.

"Nails, make up, Jenny is actually out buying you some clothes."

"So Jenny is in on this now. How's Tom with that?"

"He's okay."

But there was something in her voice. I looked at her. That moment of clarity that had struck me before was still with me. I could read her like a book.

"Well, he's a little...he's coming to grips with the fact that she grabbed your cock."

I smiled. My teeth were extra bright for the red. "Well, it was sitting right there, under the glass."

When we had breakfasted Jenny had noted that I was hard under the glass table top, and...big. And she had asked if she could touch me. It.

I hadn't said anything. Just looked at Tom.

Molly had said, "Go ahead. He won't mind."

Tom shrugged. But he was thinking about it. His wife with her hand on another man's cock. It was something to absorb.

Now, in our bedroom a couple of hours later, Jenny asked, "Well, are you ready?"

"To be made up?"

"Yep."

"Okay."

She looked down at the sink. My cock was pointing towards the faucet, big and hard.

"My, God, Jack. It's actually dripping!"

I watched as pre-cum gathered at the tip and drooled down.

"Well,"I said. "Well."

She knelt down and took me in her mouth. She worked my shaft and swirled her tongue over my head. It was so good my knees actually trembled.

She stood up. "God, Jack. Is this really making you that horny?"

It was a moment of truth time. I could deny it, and have it be an obvious lie. My pecker was bobbing, after all. Or I could admit it.

"I guess so." A couple of hours ago, before I had seen my lips, I never would have admitted to such a thing. But now...now I was a changed man. the world was opening up for me as it had never opened before.

"Well," she said. "Have a seat and let me get to work. Jenny's going to come back in a while, and I want to at least show her some progress."

Molly sat next to me at her vanity table and fitted fake nails to my digits. I don't have the gnarly mitts of people who work with machines and tools. In fact, one of my hobbies is music. Playing the guitar and the piano, and my fingers reflect that. They are long and slender. And now they grew longerer and slenderer.

Molly pushed the cuticles, trimmed and sanded. She selected some modest ovals for my first time nails, and put a dab of glue on the backs to help the natural adhesive they came with.

"These have to last a week, and I don't want you losing them," she explained.

Long lasting lipstain, long lasting nails...my wife really had this planned out.

I had never realized how delicate and intricate the hand motions required to apply make up were. I watched as she stroked down from the cuticle. Several strokes, and my nails were red. Blood red. To match my lips.

She did the next nail, and the next. She was surprisingly fast for such delicate work.

Then she put on another coat, and another.

"Three strokes down and three coats on," she mumbled, almost like a catechism. Then she put on a clear coat to preserve and protect.

"All right," she smiled happily. "These puppies will last. Get your feet up here."

"My feet?"

"They'll look so delicious, pointing out from your open toed high heels."

She had an almost evil grin on her face when she said that, and I put my feet up.

She didn't have to put fake nails on my toes, although she laughed and threatened me with them. But it did take a bit of work. Men's toenails tend to be a bit gnarly. But that just made them look super good when they were done.

"Wow!" I exclaimed. I was holding my thigh and lifting my foot so I could see them.

"Sexy, baby." She said. "Now stop admiring yourself and let me do your face."

I sat still and she leaned into me, her face close, her breath on my flesh, and began cleaning my pores. She scrubbed me clean with moisturizer, then began putting on primer. As she worked she offered explanations. "The primer makes your face a little flat, takes the color out. Makes your face into a canvas."

"So you're going to paint a picture on my face."

"Your face is going to be a picture, all right. Maybe I'll put a moo cow on your forehead. Or a birdie flying across your cheek."

"Haven't you done enough?"

"Not nearly," and she giggled. "This is foundation, gets rid of any blemishes...which you don't have. You have extremely excellent skin. We should have done this long ago."

"Why didn't you?"

"I thought about it."

That surprised me. "Really?"

"Oh, yes. Haven't you ever wondered why I make you wear your hair long? I dream of making you up and brushing your hair out, giving you a few curls...this is blush. See the color coming back?"

I could, and I said so.

"Now, the eyes. This is the delicate part. Do you want dark, smoky eyes? Or blue eyes? Or shiny eyes? What do you think is sexy?"

"Shadowy."

"Ooh. I like shadows. I'l make it look like your eyes are in caves. Staring out at the world like a dangerous animal."

Her words made me shiver and my cock bob. She laughed.

"Speaking of dangerous animals."

"Crap. I just came yesterday."

"Wait until I'm done with you. You'll be a walking cum machine. You'll spew like the world is ending."

"I think it may—"

"Honey! I'm home!" Jenny's voice drifted back to us.

Molly giggled. "What a clown," she observed, then she yelled, "Back here!"

Jenny entered the room. Tom was right behind her.

"Holy fuck!" Jenny whispered.

"My God," Tom blurted. "Your face, it's just like…just like…"

"Like a girl's," Molly spoke with satisfaction. "I told you I'm good."

"And look, his…" Jenny stopped talking. And her silence was so loud we turned and looked at her.

She was staring at my penis. Red and big and hungry, drooling, bobbing, wanting.

Molly snickered. "Told you he was big."

"Yeah, but…but…"

"Hey, babe," Tom interjected.

She looked up at him. She looked at Molly. She looked at my dick. I might not have even existed, except for my penis and, of course, the fact that I was gaining a woman's face.

She grabbed Tom and turned him around. "You and I have to talk." Her voice was actually fierce, and she walked him out of the room.

"What the heck?" I murmured.

Molly just smiled.

"Come on. Let's put some earrings on you, and some rings and bangles and stuff."

She chose a pair of medium size rings and she took out a needle and a little bottle.

"What are you doing?"

"Piercing." she examined my lobe, handled it and put the needle to it.

"I don't think—OW!"

"Shut up. You'll thank me."

Well, it didn't look like I had much choice. She pierced my other ear and set the earrings in place.

It felt weird, having the danglies caressing the side of my neck, but cool, too.

"Let's put a bone through your nose and we'll be done."

I looked at her. "No."

She grinned. "No. Maybe some other time."

"Maybe some other life."

"Ooh, did you just propose to me for another lifetime?"

I bumbled on an answer for that one, and she took my hand and dragged me out to the living room.

Tom and Jenny were sitting on the couch, facing each other, and in very close consultation. Their faces were two inches apart, and it looked like they had been discussing matters of deep import. They looked at us when we entered, and Jenny turned back to Tom. "Well?"

He sighed. Looked at me. He looked back at his wife. He almost seemed to sag as he nodded and said, "Yes."

Jenny hugged him, and planted a big smackeroo on his mouth. "You'll be so glad."

"I think it's you who will be glad," he quipped.

I wondered what they had been talking about.

"Let's dress him," stated Molly.

Jenny clapped her hands and jumped up. "Wait until you see what we got him."

I took notice of the bags then. There were a lot of them. "What'd you do? Buy the store out?"

"Don't you worry your pretty head about that," Jenny gushed. "I'm frugal, and I know my way around a sale."

"Oh."

"Doesn't he need a wig? Or something?"

The girls stood back and inspected me.

"We could try combing his hair out. It might be long enough."

"Long enough for a bob. Tom, go get my wig from the closet. And in the garage there's a foot square box. It's marked 'Aunt.' Bring that, too."

Tom stood up. He had the most interesting expression on his face. Sort of an anticipation, when he looked at me. "Okay."

Tom gone they stripped me. All the way. Not that a peignoir is much. I stood there, a slender man with a woman's face, and my cock was hard and erect and pointing and...God, was I horny.

Jenny grabbed my penis, looked down at it, and sounded like she was ready for a ten course meal. "We're going to need to do something about this."

"We?" asked Molly, a twisted grin on her face.

"Well...well..." Jenny licked her lips, then reluctantly let go of my penis.

They put a pair of panties on me, and that sure didn't work. My cock was so hard it nearly ripped the material.

"How about the corset?" Jenny asked.

"Too short."

"I've got a longer one."

At that moment Tom came back in. He was carrying the wig and a box and he put them down.

"Honey, go get my corset, the boned one, in my top drawer."

Tom nodded. He was being a good sport, just going along with it, and I wondered why. Something was not right here.

"Okay, let's put this bra on him."

Jenny took a large cupped bit of cloth out of a bag and held it out. Together they wrapped it around me, fastened it, adjusted it, and pulled it up over my shoulders.

"Now this is a real over the shoulder boulder holder," Molly giggled. "How are we going to fill this?"

Jenny went to the box, opened it and reached in. "Voila!" she bragged, and lifted a pair of breast forms up.

"Oh, my Gosh!" marveled Molly. "Where on earth?"

"My aunt had a mastectomy. Left these to remember her by."

"Well, bless your aunt."

"Bless indeed. Now, come here, sexy."

The way she called me sexy, it was...more. That's all I can say. There was something going on with Jenny. She was flustered and excited and everything, and more than just a simple make over should be. Even if I was that make over.

She shoved the big mounds into my cups, and suddenly I had a monster build. Like I say, I'm slender, except for my big belly, of course. But Tom chose that moment to arrive with the longer corset.

"Holy, fuck!" he whispered. "That's really...really.."

"Pull your tongue in, lover. She's not for you."

Molly glanced at Jenny, and there was something really significant in that glance. I didn't understand, but Molly seemed to, and she seemed to be having deep thoughts.

"Here we go," they helped me step into the garment and pulled it up. When they reached my weenie it was tough going. My pogo stick didn't want to stop jumping. Still, they pulled, and pushed, and told me to suck it in, and they managed to get the corset on me. It had a snap at the bottom and they snapped it up so I couldn't dangle, should I ever get soft.

My cock, of course, was pointed up, and I was pooched a little bit over. It hurt a little, but I could stand it.

Then came the nylons and the dress, and, finally, the high heels.

And the wig.

Done.

They put me in front of a mirror and I gasped. As well as I could considering the corset.

I was a tall woman with an hourglass shape. And a lot of hours topside.

My calves were made shapely by the high heels, and as long as I didn't try to walk I was okay. Not going to fall on my face.

My ass and my chest were flared out, courtesy of the corset, which made my hips round and my chest…you know about my chest.

Then the face. Delicately made up, shaded so the strong masculine lines of my chin were softened and rounded.

My eyes were, as she had promised, like glints in a sexy cave.

And everything was topped off by an auburn wig, long tresses waved over my shoulders.

And I knew why women get dressed up. Aside form the sexy feeling of compression, it was a turn on.

"Wow," I blurted.

"Tom, take our picture."

Tom took her cell phone and snapped pics of us. Me in the center, Molly and Jenny by my sides. I bent my knees slightly and we were all pretty much the same size.

We smiled. We aped. We had a ball. And I felt like I was…let loose. Like I had been in prison all my life, and was suddenly set free, and handed a million dollars to boot.

"Tom, go get some champagne," commanded Jenny. " Good champagne."

Dutifully, Tom headed for the liquor store.

Hunh. Why was he being so accommodating? And why was Jenny acting so weird?

But I didn't have a chance to think anymore because of a knock on the door.

We all looked at each other. I was suddenly frightened, but the girls pushed me towards the door, and I felt a profound sense of…of righteousness. I opened the door, and gaped.

Reverend Thompson stood, bible in hand, and smiled.

Reverend Thompson is old. 80 years old, and his eyesight was fading. He said, "Hi, are Molly and Jack here?"

I was flustered, started blubbering, and Molly pushed past me.

"Hi, Reverend," she stepped out and closed the door. I could hear them talking. Very pleasant.

Jenny turned to me. She held my biceps and focused her gaze on me. It was a hungry gaze and it made me nervous. "Alone at last."

She fused her body to mine. Crushed my lips with hers. I felt one of her hands go to one of my boobs. I knew she was squeezing, feeling, taking advantage of me.

"Hey, wait…I…Molly!"

She laughed, then turned serious. "Jack, I'm going to fuck your brains out. I have never been so turned on in my life. I talked to Tom and he said it's all right. This once, because you're a girl."

"But I…I…"

The door opened and Molly came back in. And stopped. And stared at us.

"Jack?" her voice was level.

I looked at her. "I didn't...she..."

Jenny said: "Molly. I am going to fuck Jack's brains out. When I am done he is going to have a bad case of the stupids."

A long minute passed. Well, it was only seconds, but it felt like minutes. Then: "Oh, is that all."

I gawped at her.

"I thought it was something serious."

"But...but..."

They both giggled, and Molly said, "Jack, I've told you that Jenny is a slut. And she told me earlier that she was going to have your cock in her or else. Well, what could I do? Right?"

"But, Tom...he..."

Tom pushed through the door at that moment. He stopped, didn't even close the door, just stared at Jenny, her arms around me, the look on Jenny and Molly's face. The look on mine.

"What's this...are you trying to fuck my wife?" His voice rose up in anger.

"But...I wasn't..."

He grinned. "Gotcha." Then he grew serious. "Only one thing, Jack."

"Uh..."

"Not in her butt. She hasn't given that to me, yet, and it's sort of reserved, if you get my drift. In fact, she promised me that if I let her fuck you then she'll fuck me. With her asshole. So...you got to do it, man."

"But...but..."

"That's right. No butt."

He and Jenny and Molly laughed then, and Molly pushed me, and Jenny guided me, and I staggered back towards the bedroom.

I've had women before. I'm not one of these guys who never had sex before marriage. In fact, I had had a LOT of sex before being married. But I had never had sex like this.

She walked me into my bedroom and closed the door. She lifted my dress, somehow managed to easily unsnap the bottom of the corset. She rolled the lip of the corset up and managed to extricate my dick.

"But, Jenny, I don't think—"

"Shush," she said. "I'm a slut, I'm in heat, and I've never had a woman."

"But..."

She kissed me. My dick was pressed into her belly, aching and throbbing and drooling.

Her mouth searched mine, our lips were as if glued together, and her tongue explored my mouth. She had her hands on my cheeks at first, then she simply grabbed my earrings and held me in place while she raped my mouth.

Oh, God, was it good! I hadn't kissed another woman than my wife for ten years, and now, to have my mouth savaged by such an expert, it was wonderful, and tender, and different and exciting.

And I thought: *I'm a woman. I...how do I act?*

But I didn't have to worry about how I was supposed to act, Jenny took care of it all for me. She took charge, pushed me back on the bed, mounted me, and I felt my cock engulfed by strange pussy.

Wonderful pussy. So soft, so engulfing. I was surrounded by her womanly flesh and could hardly breath, and it wasn't just the corset. It was the breathlessness of unbridled sex with a stranger.

Not a stranger, but she felt like a stranger. A different person.

"God, you are big," she murmured, bracing her hands on my fake chest, squeezing her hands over my mounds, bending forward to kiss me.

She began to move then, corkscrewing up and down over my shaft. Her hips tilting and pulling, settling down and doing it all over again.

"Oh, fuck!" I whispered, then I realized something. "I don't think I can cum. I just came yesterday."

"That's okay," she breathed, reaching down and fiddling with my balls. My balls that couldn't squirt. "This is for me, not you."

I laughed then. I liked the idea of being used. Of being screwed and tossed aside. And she thought she was the slut!

For long minutes she straddled me, pumping up and down, moaning, groaning, sighing and whining, and, finally, she started to climb the mountain. Her hips started to jerk, and I knew she was cumming.

"Oh, yeah....yes..." she held on to me, her pelvis twitching, then spasming. Then she collapsed, and whispered in my ear, "There is nothing like screwing a woman, is there?"

"No," I whispered back.

At that moment the door burst open and Molly and Tom burst in. They had been listening at the door and had heard Jenny climb the mountain and fall over the other side.

"Aw right! What the fuck is going on!"

"Fuck is going on!" snapped Tom, savage but grinning.

"And nobody asked us to partake. Can you believe these selfish oafs?"

"Oafs," agreed Tom. "Selfish!"

"Well, there's only one way to handle sex oafs."

She bent and opened the bottom drawer of her dresser.

Jenny sat up, curious, "What's that?"

Molly stood up and was holding a mess of straps and a dildo. A...

dildo?

I goggled as she put it on. "Jack, when I first came up with the idea of feminizing you I realized there was one thing we would have to do."

"Have to," agreed Jenny, giggling.

"Damn, dude," said Tom. "Or maybe I should say dudette."

Molly stood, legs spread, a big cock sprouting from her groin. "What do you say, Jack? Are you going to go all the way? Or have I wasted my time with you."

Jenny turned to me. "Yeah, Jack. Are you going to put out? Or are you just a bitch?"

I was speechless.

"Tom," commanded Molly. "There's a big jar of lube in the bathroom. Get it."

Tom moved to obey. He came back in the room and handed the jar to Molly. He was grinning like his face was going to split apart. "I always wondered about this. If you do it…I'll do it. Okay, Jack?"

I was caught. I was unable to speak. I couldn't believe it. The three just stood there and stared at me expectantly.

So what could I do?

I turned over and got on all fours.

"Oh, goody," mumbled Jenny. "Give me that jar. Lube yourself up."

I could hear Tom saying, "here, let me do that, and knew that he was stroking her cock, maybe even kissing her. I felt Jenny's fingers working between my crack, feeling slick, and then she was lubing me. Pushing lube into my rectum. Reaming me with her fingers.

"Oh, fuck!" I moaned. I had never felt anything so good. It felt even better than fucking. Now how could that be?

"Okay, Jack. Tome to be a woman." Molly moved between my legs. Jenny spun around on the bed and faced me. She watched my face as Molly touched her prick to my button.

"Oh, yeah," Jenny smiled as my face opened up.

I felt that penis go deep into me. I had no breath, but what was left was snatched away. I perched on the precipice of a giant dick and my world was totally and utterly blown.

She pulled back and it felt like somebody was turning me inside out.

"Wow," muttered Tom. His voice was filled with awe and jealousy.

She thrust into me, forced me forward, and Jenny chose that moment to kiss me. There I knelt, on all fours, a hard penis pushing me forward and a soft kiss stopping me. I had never imagined anything could feel this good in my life.

In and out, and my back started scrunching up, then flattening out, I pushed my butt back and twisted, giving her penis a corkscrew of a fuck.

"Oh, baby, this is good," Molly mumbled.

I looked back over my shoulder, and her face was twisted in lust, and I understood something. She was taking my male power. She was absorbing that which made me a man, and that was okay. I certainly didn't mind a wife that pounded me with her pecker, who made me feel this way. Heck, I had made her feel this way for a decade, and what was sauce for the gander is sauce for the goose.

"Oh, my God! Look!" I intuited that Tom was pointing, and Jenny looked, then lowered my head so I could see between my arms, and back to where my dick hung.

White sperm was seeping out of Mr. Happy. I was cumming. I wasn't having an orgasm, but it felt good, happy, loosy goosy, and I was being milked. Her cock was pressing on my prostate and semen was being forced out of me.

And this was okay. I couldn't cum anyway, and this warm feeling... I had an idea it was going to last for days. The cum without a cum.

Jenny lifted my face and kissed me some more. Molly slowed down and just held her position and waited for me to empty out.

"He's done," announced Tom, and she pulled slowly out.

"Oh, God!" I said, and I fell forward, sated, but not exhausted. In fact, I had never felt so alive in my life. I was wired with sex and happiness and an inner glow.

"Well, good," Molly slapped my ass. "Now we should—"

"Ahem."

The girls looked at Tom.

Jenny said, "Really?"

Molly asked, "What?"

Jenny: "He wants to screw Jack."

"Really?"

"Really. He's been trying to get me to do anal for years, and now, seeing this beautiful ass, and if Jack is willing..."

I lay there. Was I willing? I had been made into a woman, and fucked by another woman, and then fucked by a woman made into a man, sexually. So, was I willing? Could I take yet another step?

Molly slithered up next to me, turned my face towards her.

"Jack, if you don't want to I understand. But this is your friend, and you just had his wife, and I'm going to be fucking you all week long, and maybe Jenny will to—"

"I will."

"But...if you want to try it...it won't be any harder than my dick, and it will be real flesh. Would you like to experience real flesh, Jack?"

Oh, God. What could I do? What could I say? These were my friends, and they meant so much to me. I struggled to my hands and knees and waited.

END

Full Length Books from Gropper Press

MY HUSBAND'S FUNNY BREASTS

It's not so funny when
it's happening to you!

GRACE MANSFIELD

Tom Dickson was a happy camper. He lived a good life, had a beautiful wife, then he started to grow breasts, his hair grew long, and his body reshaped. Now Tom is on the way to being a woman, and he doesn't know why.

This book has forced feminization, cross dressing, hormones, gender transformation, pegging and breast growth.

My Husband's Funny Breasts

They Made Him a Sissy!

Please, dear…don't make me do that!

PART ONE

"What is a penis for?"

I stared at my wife. "What?"

"It's not a hard question. Just answer it. What is a penis for?"

We were in the bedroom getting ready for bed. She was cleaning goop off her face and I was hanging up my pants. I stopped, mid hang, and faced her.

"What kind of a question is that?"

"It's a good and honest question. What's the good and honest answer?"

Lannie is a babe. Long, dark hair, glittering eyes, and…there is something in her, a twist, something that makes her different.

"A penis," I pontificated, "Is good for reproduction and—"

"Stop!"

"Huh?"

"It's good for reproduction."

"That's what I said. And—"

"Nope."

"What the heck are you doing?" I was getting irritated with her haughty stoppages.

"You're trying to give me all that other nonsense."

"What nonsense?"

"That a penis is necessary for pleasure."

"Well, it is!"

"Nonsense."

I went over to her. I pulled my tighty whiteys down. My pecker sprang right out. "So you're saying this doesn't give you pleasure?"

"It's not important what it does. What is important is what it is designed for.

Reproduction, urination and fun!" I almost shouted.

"Reproduction. When we have kids we need it. Urination. Yep. It's necessary. But…fun?" She tilted her head and gave me a lock of mockery. "Fun?"

"Yes! Fun!"

"Nonsense. Your penis is not necessary to the act of having fun. It is not necessary that you masturbate like a dirty, little boy, or that you sate your lustful desire in my gentle vagina."

We glared at each other. She had had some loopy ideas in the past.

We had spent a month eating nothing but raw meat, that was real fun. And going barefoot everywhere, oh, that was a large charge. But…what was she saying?

"What, my lovely wife, are you suggesting?"

"I am saying, plain and simple, that unless your penis is proposing a child, it is not going to get inside my little pleasure palace. I am saying that you should not masturbate. You should save your little peeny for the more important things in life."

"Like pissing and…and…that's all?"

"That's it."

There was a spare chair next to her vanity table and I turned it around and sat in it. "And what brought you to this bizarre conclusion?"

"Common sense."

"What's common about not fucking?"

"First, I believe that your heart only beats so many times in your lifetime, and you should conserve your beats, avoid excitement—"

"The excitement of sex," I blurted.

"—and you will live longer. Furthermore, I believe that your heart can only pump so many gallons, then it wears out. I don't want that to happen to you."

"Anything else?"

"Yes. Your penis is only good for so many squirts, then it wears out. runs down. Empties out. Whatever you want to call it."

"What?" My voice actually squeaked.

"So we need to limit your squirts, slow the flow of blood, and calm your poor heart down."

"This is ridiculous."

"You are already upset. I want you to take deep breaths and calm down."

"Like you?"

"Like me." She breathed out slowly and closed her eyes.

"And what about your pussy?" I asked. "Is your pussy on a diet?"

"I will limit sex. I will only pee. I will treat my vagina like the sacred chamber it is."

"This is ridiculous."

"And I don't want you jacking off or lusting after other women."

"This is crazy. So we can throw out your vibrator, right?"

She opened her eyes and frowned. "My vagina has special needs. I have more hormones than you, and hormones can make a girl excited. A quick session with a vibrator reduces all that stress."

"A quick…oh, my God! Are you listening to yourself?"

"It is better that you listen to me. I am trying to conserve your energies, preserve your life, and enable you to live to a ripe old age."

"If I can't have sex I don't want to live to a ripe, old age."

"Nevertheless," she stated emphatically. "You will."

Now, I don't know about you, but being told I can't have something makes me want it all the more. And being told I can't have sex resulted in the biggest boner in the history of the world, and maybe in the history of boners.

Lannie placed a hand on my knee and looked me in the eyes. "Honey, Ron, you will thank me."

"When I am laying on my death bed, after a lo-o-ong life of sexual frustration, I am suppose to thank you."

She nodded, was satisfied. "Yes."

We went to bed, and life went on, but it was a very different life.

I hadn't had a cum for a week before she laid down the law, and I was very horny. I was so horny that I became, rather quickly, desperate.

I would wake up in the morning and look at her bountiful body, the large breasts, and I wanted to attack, penetrate, pump and relieve. Instead, I would slink to the bathroom, and a shower, and try not to soap my cock.

I am not a fan of masturbation. In fact, the day I discovered that girls were built different than boys I gave up masturbating. Except for when I really had to. Which, I hate to admit, was a lot.

But I had eventually put masturbation aside, and was proud of that feat.

But when I came home I had been hard all day, distracted by the feeling of my pecker poking outward, and my balls were ready to pop. She invariably greeted me at the door with a kiss—sometimes a scorcher of a kiss, because she was horny, too—and my penis would struggle and fight against the confines of my tighty whiteys.

Going to bed was a real thrill. I would see her undress, expose that voluptuous body, those amazing breasts, and my penis would pound so hard I was afraid I would have a heart attack.

"Honey, my heart is racing. A little sex would relieve it."

"Nonsense," my most unfavorite word in the world, "just have a little patience. And discipline. Now come over here and rub my back."

That's right. My testicles are so full I groan if they even brush against my thighs, and she wants me to sit atop her buns and rub her back. Her naked back. Her bare flesh tantalizing me. My penis laying between her bare globes, dying to get inside her and…

"Can't you control that thing?" she groused. "Can't you have discipline? Like me?"

A weak sob escaped me and she looked over her shoulder at me, then sighed loudly. She lay back down and muttered, "You are so hopeless."

Hopeless was right. And helpless. And miserable. And horny. Then I had a bright idea.

"Honey, let me give you a full body rub tonight."

"Okay," she smiled. She loved the oil and the time and sensations of me loving every part of her body.

And I intended to love her vagina. Heh heh.

So I laid a big towel down on the bed, got out the oil and began rubbing. I smoothed oil into her back, I rubbed my fingers into her flesh. I made circling motions and laced my way down her body. I spent a lot of time on her butt, pressing and palpating and squeezing.

She sighed and loved it.

I went down her legs, feeling her perfect skin with my hands, feeling her relax more and more, and I knew she was getting more and more receptive to the feel of my hands on her.

My poor penis, however, was suffering for this. It was a stiff rod that kept sliding along her body, or poking into her flesh, which just made her giggle. "Don't you get too excited now, Ron."

"Don't worry, honey. I'm working on my discipline, just like you. Now turn over and let me do your front.

She rolled over and I was presented with her mammoth mounds, her shaved pubic area, her arcs and curves of lovely flesh.

I began at her feet and worked up. Pressed my fingers into her muscles and made her relax more and more.

Up to her thighs, grabbing them and stroking, letting my fingers come closer and closer to her pussy.

"Oh, yeah. Babe. You have to do this every night."

"You got it," I promised, and in my mind: *until you cum!*

I was careful around her groin. I couldn't just leap in and fuck her clit with my hand, I had to work around it. I rubbed the edges of her womanly triangle. I pressed firmly with my fingers, dragged them around her hole, and she breathed deeper and deeper. At one point I got a little too close and she gasped.

But she didn't tell me to stop.

Up to her breasts. Her mountains of pleasure, and I molded them and shaped them. I pulled on the nipples with my fingers, and she was so relaxed she didn't say anything when I took a nipple in my mouth and began to suck it.

She groaned.

I massaged her pussy area. Getting closer and closer. Pretty soon I would be able to push those legs apart. Pretty soon she would get so horny she would forget about this stupid pussy diet. Pretty soon—

"AHHHH....YES!!!! FUCK!"

Her hips rose upward, snapped upward, and I could see all her muscles tightening. Damn! She was having an orgasm! That wasn't supposed to happen! I needed to get into her!

She sagged. "Oh, thank you, honey."

"But..." I put my hands between her legs and pushed lightly.

She spun around and sat up and glared at me. "No! Bad Ron!"

"But...but...honey!"

"You are not supposed to use your penis for pleasure!"

"But you just had pleasure with your pussy!"

"That was an accident. And I suspect that you planned this! You deliberately gave me this back rub just to get inside me!"

"But I didn't—"

"So, no! You are not cumming! I've got more hormones, and if I need a little outercourse then that's okay. But you don't have hormones...so you don't need any of that silly sex stuff!"

"But you do!"

She paused, I could see her doing the math, and she folded her arms under those amazing breasts, pushing them out further, and stated, "Yes."

"So you get to cum and I don't."

"Women don't spew their seed all around. They don't empty their balls. I am in no danger of running out of semen, So, yes. I get to cum."

"And I don't."

"No."

"ARGH!" I jumped up and actually ran around in a small circle.

"So just stop throwing your little baby tantrum and come to bed."

I couldn't go to bed then, however. I was too worked up. My penis was too worked up. It was stiff and pointing and now it was actually dripping.

"Look! You're making a mess! You're dripping on the floor!"

"I don't care!"

"Well you'd better care! You'd better start behaving yourself or... or..."

"Or what? You'll stop having sex with me?"

Now she was starting to get mad. All her talk of being calm, and then having her own squirt...she was getting mad.

"I'll make you wear a chastity device!"

"You will not!"

"I will! And that will calm you down and get you under control!"

She was on her feet now, and her voice was rising up.

"I don't need to be under control! I just need a little sex!"

"And you'll get little sex! Very little!"

And we argued and argued and argued, and I finally wound up sleeping in the den.

But not sleeping in the den. Lying awake with my aching, throbbing penis. Moaning and groaning with frustration. My balls so tender. My dick dripping all over my thighs and getting me all wet.

And I'm not going to tell you all the bad thoughts I had that night. I love my wife and I will not speak ill of her.

Even though she is so damned frustrating I was thinking my nutsack as going to explode!

I woke up the next morning and was dazed with lust. And lack of sleep.

She woke up, on the other hand, and came out of our bedroom fresh and rested. Chipper. Of course, she had had a wonderful orgasm.

"Good morning, my beautiful husband."

"Good morning," I muttered.

"Oh, cheer up. Today is another day, and you've got all day to be happy!"

"There's only one thing that will make me happy."

"Oh, tut tut! Just relax and be happy. Now I'm going to go to the gym. I feel wonderful, and I need to work off some of this energy."

She headed out for the gym and I was left to my own devices.

Naked, unable to get my boner into pants, I fixed breakfast. I ate. I did the dishes. I went into the den and watched porn.

Well, of course I did! I was desperate! I needed...something!

So I watched men with big dongs plumb women with big breasts and my cock grew bigger and bigger. So bigger that I actually gave a sob or two. Or three or four. Just, the sight of so much pulchritude being wallowed in so freely, so joyously, it was too much.

I turned off the computer and sat in the dark room.

Lannie arrived home. Cheerful as all get out. She breezed past the den, then backed up and looked in. "Oh, there you are. Honey, could you make me some toast and jam? And a little hot chocolate?"

Then she was gone on down the hallway. Tripping blithely to a shower. To wash that stupendous figure, to caress those massive mammary glands, to feel her hands smoothing down her luscious legs, to...I stood up and hurried to the kitchen. I had to take my mind off Lannie. I had to do something to get my mind off my throbbing penis.

I popped some toast into the toaster, heated up some water and got out the hot chocolate. I buttered and jellied the toast and put the plate on the table. Then I stood there, leaning against the counter, looking out the window, and considered my situation.

I needed to masturbate. I hadn't done that since I was a kid, but I needed to do that now. A man has to get some relief, or his balls will turn blue, purple, and then black.

Lannie came into the kitchen and plopped down at the table. "Ooh, goody," she munched into a piece of toast, then looked up at me. "Thank you, honey, but could you go put some clothes on? You look a little silly sitting there with your penis dripping and all."

I turned to her. "Honey, I can't even get my pants on. My dick is priapic, it won't go down. All I can do is stay nude as long as you're going to make me suffer."

Chewing her little bites, she observed, "Now you know I'm doing this so you will live a full and glorious life. I just don't understand why you can't be more like me."

"Well, I can't. I need relief. I need..." I actually started to tear up.

"Oh, honey. I know it's tough. And maybe I can help you."

"You can?"

"Of course I can. That's what wives are for, right? To help their husbands?"

"Well, uh..."

"Now you do the dishes and I'll go see about helping you out."

She smiled, patted my cheek, and headed for the bedroom.

Oh, visions of sugar plums and fairies or whatever that stupid song or poem is. I was going to get a little!

I smiled. I waited, and gave her two minutes to get ready for me. I sauntered down the hallway, swaggered, actually, cock of the walk, ready to do the deed and—

"Here you go," Lannie stepped out of the bedroom and handed me a bundle of cloth.

"What the heck?" I shook it out and blinked. It was Lannie's muumuu. A dress! A freakin' billowy dress! She got it at a thrift shop and wore it when the weather was hot and she didn't feel like wearing real clothes. She wore it around the pool sometimes. But it was a dress!

"What is this?"

"You have to put some clothes on. You're a distraction."

"I'm not going to wear a dress!"

"You will if you want to cover up that peeny of yours. And, by the way, I have some ladies coming by today, and if you know what's good for you..."

"I'm not. wearing this! They'd all laugh at me! I'd be the laughing stock of town!"

"Nonsense. But, do what you want. But you either hide in the basement, or you wear this."

"I'll close the door and stay in the den."

"This is an official Society Meeting. We're going to need the computer."

"But you can't...I don't want to...you need to..." I ran out of things that I was too befuddled to say anyway.

"The meeting takes place at one. Do what you want. I'm going to get ready."

She returned to the bedroom and I was left holding this flimsy bit of rag. A damned muumuu! What the hell!

I walked into the bedroom after her. "Lannie. this has got to stop."

She was sitting at her vanity table, making up her face, and I was forced to watch her become even more beautiful."

"I sort of like the way things are. I enjoyed breakfast, I had a wonderful night last night...I like the way things are going."

"But I am suffering!"

"Nonsense. Men go without cumming all the time. What if you were a monk, or a had an accident and couldn't use your peter? You would just learn to deal with it. So just learn to deal with it.

She ran a tube over her lips and my cock gave an extra shuddery bounce. I was a sucker for juicy, red lips.

She noticed and smiled at me. "Would you like a little lipstick?"

I jumped back. "No!"

"Suit yourself." She went back to coloring her lips, then smacked loudly. "Personally, I think red lipstick is the only way to go. What do you think?"

"ARGH!" I stomped out of the room.

It was twelve thirty. Half hour to bitch time, as I liked to call it. A half hour, or less, until the old biddies started showing up. Of course they weren't all old biddies. There was Jane, from down the street. World class knockers, and always joking. Then there was Sandra Smith, she had a killer body and a killer face, and when she talked she moved her lips like she was trying to kiss you. And there was...crap! I had to stop this! I was just making myself more hornier.

I walked into the den. I could lock the doors, but they were pretty flimsy. If Lannie so much as pushed on them they were liable to give way.

I went back into the bedroom and tried to put some jeans on. God, what a struggle, bent my dick every which way but loose, but I couldn't get them on. Not without suffering 'bent-dickitis.'

I went back to the den and picked up the lap top. Then I went back to the bedroom and picked up the balled up muumuu. I had thrown it in a corner, but I needed it.

I was afraid some of those women would want to come down to the basement.

"That's a boy," murmured Lannie.

"Argh!" I answered, then I headed for the basement.

It was cool in the basement, and I headed for the easy chair.

We had once had dreams of making the basement into a giant playroom, and we had even started construction. There was a side room with a massage table in it. The main room had a pool table set up, and a ping pong table was folded and shoved into a corner.

There were also tools, material for building walls and cabinets, and a complete sound system that had never been set up.

I put the laptop down on the table next to the easy chair and held out the muumuu. For Heysoos's sake. I pulled the thing over my head and let it drape down.

It was sheer and billowy. You could see through it, but it was gossamer material, and as it slid over my cock it felt so-o-o good. I grabbed my penis and rubbed, and was on the edge rea-a-ally fast.

I let go. I didn't want to be a jacker offer. There was just something so…immature…about throttling your weenie until it spits.

So I sat there in my muumuu and watched porn.

I heard the women upstairs. Mumbling voices, giggling laughter, the tap, tap of their heels.

I sank deeper into my funk. I was horny. I needed relief. What was wrong with that?

Nothing!

I had been fucking for years, and it hadn't hurt me. And people had been fucking since before the first baby was born!

So why should I be a monk?

Why should I be allowed into my wife's pussy, eh?

I married her! I have certain rights, didn't I?

The women upstairs went on with their meeting all afternoon. Blah, blah, blah.

I could imagine their silly nonsense, talking about their families and their children and grandchildren.

Then I had a thought. Was Lannie acting this way because of her Ladies…what was it…oh, yeah. Sissy. The Ladies' Sissy Society?

Had they infected her with some nonsense about men and women and feminism and females needing more rights and all that?

I had a feeling they had.

I looked over to the fridge, and I remembered: We had beer in there! We had just started on the basement, I think I had dreams of it being a 'super man cave,' and I had bullied a fridge down the steps and filled it with beer.

I stood up, my weenie brushing against the thin material and making me shiver, and walked to the fridge. I opened it, and smiled.

The top shelf had row upon row of dark bottles. Beer for the masses, like Coors and Budweiser.

The second shelf had Pacifico, Corona, and other types of beer. Made in Mexico mostly, and without the GMO and other stuff that Americans put in their beer.

The third shelf, right above the vegetable drawers, however, was the gold mine. Tire Biter, Landshark, and…OMG! Golden Monkey! I actually had a six pack of Golden Monkey!

Golden Monkey was my beer of choice when I wanted to lose my senses quickly. One beer made your eyes cross. Two beers made your eyes move independently. Three beers and one eye did a polka and the other did a cancan. Four beers and you'd actually believe the election wasn't rigged.

Grinning, finally a cure for my priapism in hand, I popped a top and did the chug a lug.

Mmm. Golden Monkey is sweet with a slight taste to it. Some people don't like the taste. I don't, but the effects of the beer were worth it. I went back to my easy chair and listened to the racket upstairs.

Crazy women. Thinking men should do without. Closing their legs like they thought they were better than us. They probably all jacked off.

One beer gone.

Or jilled off, I thought, as I began drinking the second bottle.

Jilled off each other. I giggled at the idea. Women with pussies doing each other when a perfectly good man, a cock, was at hand. Didn't they understand? Men and women had been doing the dirty since before there was dirt! It was no time to start…hmmm. Now how did that bottle get empty?

Two beers gone.

Probably jilled off everything. Jilled off their children, their pets. And never let their husbands get any. Jilled off their aunts and uncles, and their poor husbands suffered. Walked funny because they were so stiff and there wasn't any relief. Jilled off their parents and their grandparents. Jilled off passersby on the street. Jilled off the cops who tried to arrest them and the firemen who tried to douse them with water. Jilled the mailman for a letter and the waiter for a tip. Jack and Jill went up the hill with a bucket and a quarter. Jill came back with two fifty… they didn't go up for water.

I turned the bottle upside down and ascertained…yep. Dead soldier. Jilled to death. Here lies a victim of women's underwear. Uh, women's everywhere. A victim. Like this empty bottle. How the fuck did that happen?

I opened a fourth bottle. I had never drunk so much Golden Monkey in my life. Hell, two bottles and I couldn't pass a drunk test. What were they testing drunks for, anyway? Who cares how smart a drunk is?

Not like me, who was smart all the time. Not like me—glug—who can hold his liquor.

I couldn't hear anything upstairs, but I didn't care. What I cared about was this bottle. In my hand. Half gone. And I remembered a story from college. Not a story, an actual happening. Friend of mine named Dave shoved a bottle of beer up his ass and got so drunk he couldn't stand up. On one beer.

Apparently alcohol goes right through the membrane of the colon and right into the system and you get super drunk super fast.

Wouldn't that be interesting? Fuck myself in the ass with a bottle of

Golden Monkey? How drunk would I get? I mean, I had had lotsh of bottlesh all ready. Surely one more couldn't helf.

Couldsh it?"

Hmmm.

I looked at the bottle.

Only a little left in it. Like half. Surely that much alcohol wouldn't bother me. Not now. Heck. I had proved my resishtance. A little drinkie poo up the poo poo would be nothing for a man like me. Right?

So I struggled around, leaned over the arm of the chair, and tried to fit the bottle to my ass.

Normally, I don't think there's a chance in hell of me getting a bottle up my ass. I'm a tight ass. I never put anything up there.

But now I was drunk, and relaxed, and…loose.

The bottle popped into my hole and I heard the gurgle of liquid passing.

Sort of like gas passing, but it was liquid passing, but the wrong way. What?

I struggled to my feet, and I didn't really know who I was or where I was or anything. I just knew the world was spinning and I had to get out of there.

The basement was closetphobic. The stairs were a way to heavin'. Uh, heaven.

I staggered across the floor and up the stairs. I opened the door and staggered out into…

The Ladies' Sissy Society was having a quiet moment. Everybody was listening to a very important message from somebody. Syphilis or somebody.

I had my dress up over my head, a beer bottle coming out of my ass, and I belched. Except the belch was sort of solid. Right over the leader of the Ladies' Sissy Society. All over her. Matthilda somebody.

"Oh! Schuse me!" I tried to brush her off, and smeared the deadly toxins into her. Her dress was ruined, her hair was a mess, everybody was screaming…so I barfed again. I had drunk a lot of Golden Monkey, and I had a lot of Golden Barf stored up.

"Ron!" My wife shrieked.

I barfed on her.

"Help!" A lady yelled, and tried to run across the living room to the front door. I hit her halfway across the room. Projectiled her. And she fell over.

Oh, my, I thought. *I guess I puke hard.*

Ladies slipping and falling in the upchuck. Dresses and faces dripping with vomit. Women shrieking for help, screaming, running around and trying to scrape vomitus off themselves.

Matthilda was sitting on the couch, wiping puke off her chest. She was low cut and it was dripping and slipping between her awesome boobies.

My wife was crying—now what was she crying for?—and my tossed up Golden Monkey was all over her legs.

Screeching, crying, sobbing, puked on ladies.

And I didn't understand it. Heck, I didn't have a drop on me.

Then, the room swirling about me, I tried to sit down. And fell down. And I looked up at the fan, whirling above me. Going round and round. And I watched that fan. The blades, and they slowed down, and then I was the one going around and around. The fan blades were still. In relationship to me. And it was the room that was spinning. Spinning. Spin...snore.

PART TWO

"Wha..." I looked around blearily. I was standing up. Well, I was sagging from something, but held upright. What was going on?

"Wha happen...?"

Everything was dark. Oh, my God! I was dead! My eyes were dead and I couldn't see anything!

"Help!" I asked, almost conversationally.

Wait a minute, I had heard my own voice, so I wasn't dead. At least, my voice wasn't dead.

"Help!" I asked a little louder.

My voice ricocheted a bit, and I knew where I was.

I opened my eyes.

Yep.

I was in the basement.

And I was hanging! I struggled, my feet were numb, but I managed to get them under me and push up. I stood, and realized that I was chained up. I was being held against the basement wall, which was cement, by chains.

Why? What was happening?

"Help!" I yelled. And I heard noises above me. The scraping of a chair, the tap tap of feet. Not two feet, but many feet.

Then the door to the kitchen opened and a small bit of light filtered down to me.

"Hello? Lannie? Somebody? Help me!"

Feet clicking on the stairs, then the lights went on. I blinked, and looked around.

Yes, I was chained to the basement wall. Several eye bolts had been sunk into the cement, and the chains kept me upright.

I looked down, I had no clothes on. My penis was, of course, sprouting. Of course it was. I hadn't had any sex in ages, and my balls, they felt so big down there. Big and ripe, like melons ready to burst. I had never been so exquisitely sensitive in my life.

I looked over to where Lannie was descending the stairs. Lannie and...several other pairs of legs came into view. Sexy legs. Beautiful legs. Legs all calf curvy and going up, up, to well shaped, rounded buttocks.

"Lannie?"

She was in full view now, striding towards me. Naked, those incredible boobs on proud display, an angry look on her face.

I was confused. What had I done to piss her off? I should be the one pissed off. She had closed her legs and I hadn't had any for the longest time!

Men need to cum! They deserve to cum! They—

"I hope you're proud of yourself!"

"Honey, I...what's happening? Why am I chained to this wall?"

"As if you didn't know!"

I looked behind her, the ladies of The Ladies' Sissy Society were behind her. They were also naked. They just stood there and glowered at me. Anger on their faces, boobs out thrust, totally pissed off.

"Lannie? Honey? I don't know what you're talking about! What have I done, and what are all these...these ladies doing here? Don't you know I'm...I'm naked, and...and..." I was too embarrassed to point out that my dick was pointing out. Heck, it was obvious.

"You really don't remember?" She didn't believe that, and that was for sure.

"Remember what?"

"Jocelyn," Lannie raised a hand and one of the women behind her put a cell phone on it.

"You really don't remember...so take a look."

She tapped her finger on the phone a couple of times, then turned so I could see.

It was a meeting, the meeting they had been having, and they had videod the thing. Matthilda was sitting and talking about how men must be brought to heel, how they must learn their places, that they should— suddenly the door behind her burst open and my eyes widened. I burst into the room, the muumuu up around my neck, my penis big and purple and out of control. I could see bits of semen flick off it as I whirled about, and then I could see the bottle in my ass.

Oh, my God! I had had a bottle in my ass?

Then I focused on the women shrieking and trying to get out of the way, and I was puking, puking here, puking there, puking everywhere, spewing an endless amount of guts.

And the women were being splattered with goo and they shrieked. They ran all over the place, but they stepped in my vomit and upended. Their feet went up and their dresses slid back and all I saw was panties and puke and myself dancing here and dancing there, drunkenly, saying things, and puking, puking more and more.

Then, the worst, I stopped moving around and throwing up. I held up my penis and started pissing. I was mumbling and shouting weird things about cleaning them off, and I pissed on the crying, screaming ladies.

Then the video was over.

My face was slack and my eyes were round. My mouth was open in shock.I was stunned.

I had weird images floating through my mind, like a memory, but it was all so unreal. Surely that couldn't have been me!

No. It was a doppelgangere, an alien from another universe. He had stolen my body and...and...

I looked at Lannie. The look in her eyes crushed me. I had shamed her, betrayed her. And, worse, I knew that there was no chance in hell of me ever cumming in her again as long as I lived. Maybe not even after I had lived.

"Now do you remember?" she sneered.

"I...I don't...did I...that couldn't have been—"

Matthilda stepped forward and slapped my face.

"You...you...MAN!" she cursed me. "We of The Ladies Sissy Society don't believe in violence, but right now...grrr...right now I am sore tried!"

The other women in the room were making a growling sound, muttering dire imprecations, threatening me with what they wanted to do to me.

"Tar and feather him!"

"Ride him out of town on a rail!"

"Cut off his weenie!"

"Wait!" I screamed. "I'm sorry! I didn't know what I was doing!" That threat, to cut off my weenie, was terrifying. These women were obviously out of control.

In front of me Lannie started to cry. "I cook and clean for you. I perform oral sex! I even let you put your penis in my vagina. Well, bub, those days are past!"

"But, honey, I didn't...that wasn't really me...you know..."

Matthilda pushed past her and put a strap around my head. Behind her other women were consoling Lannie.

"Hey! Hey! I—ghueoldk!" My voice was muffled as a gag was stuffed into my mouth. What was worse...it was a penis gag! It was a little penis and I could feel it in my mouth, like a real dick!"

"Ronald Simpson. We of The Ladies Sissy Society will now adjourn to the upstairs...where we will discuss your case and an appropriate punishment."

With that, me struggling and trying to speak, all those naked women turned and tromped across the floor, up the stairs, and into the living room.

I was left alone, chained to the wall, to contemplate my crimes.

I pulled on the chains. They rattled, but were firm. One of those ladies knew how to sink a bolt in cement. And the chains...no way I was going to bust them.

I examined the straps on my wrists and ankles. Tough leather, with a band of metal running around the backs of them. Thick. No weaknesses in any joint. I was affixed to the wall as surely as a butterfly is pinned to a corkboard.

Upstairs I could hear voices. Women muttering angrily.

Oh, God! Had I really done all that? I sort of remembered things, bits of images, but…it was all so…but then…Golden Monkey will do that.

That's right. If I was guilty of any crime it was Golden Monkey's fault.

About an hour later one of the women came into the basement.

"Hey! I'm sorry!" I yelped around the penis gag. My voice was muffled, but understandable.

She sniffed, and rummaged through a metal shelf I had placed against the far wall.

"Did you hear me?"

She didn't say anything. She bent at the knee and examined the things on the lower shelves.

"What are you going to do to me?"

Silence, and she stood up and was holding something.

"What are you looking for?"

She turned and I saw…the hat. My beer hat. It was a hat with a set up or hold a big can of beer. A flexible straw ran down to my mouth. It was a joke and I had never used it.

"What do you need that for? What's going on?"

She waked past me, didn't deign to even look at me, the beer hat in her hand.

"Hey! Say something! Tell my wife I need to talk to her! Tell her I'm sorry! Hey! Hey!"

Then she was out of the basement, and she had turned off the lights.

Damn. I just stood there, unable to move without clinking. I was getting tired. What was up with those women? I mean, yeah, I had gotten sick, but that was no reason for them to treat me like this. Right?

I stood there in the darkness, and I felt weak. I was tired, I was hungry, and I was hung over.

Had I really done all that? Puked on all those women?

I guessed I had. I had seen the video, after all.

And standing there, in the gloom of the basement, thinking about it, I giggled.

The way they had run, and fallen and been slopped with puke. Bunch of stuck up bitches, and I started to laugh.

Then I stopped. This wasn't funny. I needed to get loose.

The door to the upstairs opened and another woman came down the stairs. She was holding my beer hat in her hands.

"Hey! You have to let me go! this is illegal. This is false imprisonment!"

She ignored me, walked towards me, took the penis gag out of my mouth. Before I could say anything, however, she placed the beer hat on my head. She stuck the tube in my mouth and said, "It's the only food you'll get, so don't let go of the straw.

She turned and walked away, and I tasted…baby food!

WTF? Baby food?

I almost spit the straw out, but I was hungry, and there was nothing else on the menu, and these bitches were really crazy. They might never feed me again.

The lights went out, and I stood in the darkness, baby food drizzling down my throat, and I really felt bad.

Sure, it wasn't nice of me to puke on everybody, and then to piss on them. But that was all a mistake! They didn't have to treat me like this!"

Another hour passed. I finished the baby food and spit the straw out. Gah. Well, it wasn't bad. But it was still baby food!

Another hour, and the door opened, the lights went on, and four ladies and my wife tromped down the stairs. They were still naked, and I had recovered enough from my hangover and hunger that my dick bounced a little.

Yeah, baby. You can't keep a good man down.

They lined up in front of me. A row of thrusting bosoms. Man, I had forgotten how horny I was, but it was coming back to me now.

"Ronald Simpson, we of The Ladies' Sissy Society have decided on a punishment."

I stared at them, my cock bobbing. Somehow none of them looked down at it. I heard a little splattering sound and realized that I was dripping.

"Your punishment is…'The Hook.' You will be in the hook until you have cleaned up the mess you have made. Further, you will clean the house and person of every woman you have defiled. So let it be written, so let it be true."

Man, they must have gotten that last out of the Moses movie.

Then they started moving on me, and things suddenly weren't so funny.

First, one of them grabbed my dick and pulled it. I arched out from the wall. Damn woman had a grip!

"Lannie!" I begged.

She stood in front of me, watching, anger in her eyes.

"I can't believe you shamed me. You brought this on yourself."

"But…but…"

"Pull his dick down. Push his hips back. That's it, a little more…"

PHWWUT! There was no sound except that in my head, but that

sound was the sound of the Titanic ripping open. I felt a steel rod go up my rear. It was shaped like a 'J', and they snugged it tight, putting me on my tip toes. Then they tied a rope to the eye on the top of the J, and pulled a rope up to my neck. They put a collar around my neck and attached the rope to a ring located at the back of my neck. Suddenly I was arched, on top toes, and I couldn't lower myself. I was hoisted. Totally and truly hoisted.

Mind you, it didn't feel bad. Just...awkward.

Then the ladies put a belt around my waist. It had straps that went down under my buns and up. They cinched it tight, then loosened one of my hands.

"Careful, now."

I tried to struggle, and for a second it looked like I could get my hand free, but the girl holding my pecker squeezed. Hard. I stopped my struggling.

Then my wrist was attached to a chain on the belt. I could move my hand about a foot and a half, but that was all. I certainly couldn't pull the hook out of myself.

Then they did my other hand.

Then they put hobbles on my ankles and I could only take little, mincing steps.

Matthilda stepped back and faced me. The other girls, now giggling and with big smiles on their faces.

"This is a sissy trainer. Though you have shown no inclination to be a sissy, it is still useful in bringing you to a proper frame of mind."

"Let me go," I gasped. I was arched and my butt was sticking up.

"You will find that it is awkward, but not terribly painful. Unless, of course, you try to remove it. You can't roll or jump or contort in any way to get the butt hook out of your ass."

"Why are you doing this?"

"We will let you out of the Sissy Butt Hook when you have cleaned the houses of the ladies you defiled, and accomplished any other 'act' they wish you to perform.

There was something funny about the way she said 'act,' but I didn't pick up on that.

"So, are you ready to begin making amends for the terrible thing you did?"

"Uh..." I looked around. They looked at me. They waited.

So what was I going to do? Say no, and stay in this infernal torture device?

"Okay."

I tell ya, Mrs. Simpson's son was feeling pretty low about then.

"Very well. Come upstairs and receive your first instructions."

They turned and marched off. Up the stairs, and I was left alone.

With a hook up my butt, immoveable and causing me to arch my back and tip toe.

So, with arched back, looking like a Sissy, I walked across the cement floor, and tried to mount the stairs.

Oh, God! I couldn't lift my foot high enough. Steps are about 7 inches up, and by the time my foot raised to six inches I felt shooting pains in my butt, and pleasure. Incredible, soul numbing pleasure. Pleasure that made my balls tighten up and my pecker drip.

I lowered my foot. I raised my foot. Oh, fuck! I lowered my foot.

I tried to walk up the steps backwards, but my feet were slanted because I was on tip toe, and my heel slid off.

I tried to bend over, and could do it, I could get to my knees, but I couldn't get up the stairs on all fours like that.

I struggled to my feet and turned sideways, and that worked. I was able, if I was very careful, and held the rail with one hand, to sidle up the steps.

Step by step I struggled, inch by inch I went up the stairs, and, finally, I reached the top step. I turned my whole body and grabbed the knob, twisted, and walked into the room.

The ladies were still there. Most of them. They had been laughing and chatting, and they suddenly went silent.

"What...what do you want me to do?"

"Clean the house," snapped Lannie.

I tell ya, I was too beat to complain, to resist. I nodded my head and headed for the pantry. Inside the pantry was a shelf with rags and cleaning supplies. I grabbed spray bottles and rags and headed back to the living room.

I had really done a job. I had puked simply everywhere. And it hadn't helped that the ladies, except for a few towels placed so they could sit, hadn't done anything. They had just let the puke dry, so it was caked on everything. Furniture, tables, the floor.

They continued chatting as if I wasn't there.

I sprayed furniture and wiped, and then found I was going to have to get a bucket of water and really soap the furniture down and rinse it.

I went to the kitchen, managed to bend enough to get a bucket, and struggled to lift it over the lip of the sink. I filled it, put some soap in it, and carried back out to the living room.

"And he actually had the nerve to want sex. After I had expressly told him no, and that it was for his own good."

She was talking about me. I didn't say anything, I just went about cleaning the living room.

"Honestly," one of the women answered Lannie. "I don't see how you put up with it."

Scrub, scrub. I used a brush. I washed everything again and again, and finally got all trace of puke out of the furniture.

And had to do the rug.

Sighing, my body sore, my butt hole hoisted and groaning with a mix of a little pain and a lot of pleasure, I went for the vacuum cleaner.

"He's very good at oral, however…"

The ladies looked at me.

"Really?"

"Absolutely. Try him out when he cleans your house, if you want."

There were nods and smiles, and I said, "I need to run the vacuum."

"Don't let us stop you," snapped one of the women. All the smiles disappeared, turned into frowns.

I vacuumed, and, good news, our vacuum is a good one. It managed to suck up nearly everything. I still had to get down on my hands and knees, a feat if there ever was one, and scrub the place, but…thank God for good vacuums.

Then I started polishing woodwork. I pranced around the room with a can of spray and one of the girls giggled. "Stop."

I stopped. I faced her. I was about as low as a man could get, but she was about to put me a little lower.

"Lannie? Do you have heels?"

All the ladies giggled, and Lannie left the room. When she came back she was holding a pair of her high heels. She bent down and put them on my feet, then stood back and smiled. Her mouth was twisted in pleasure.

And, small joy, the heels actually gave me a little support. I could relax my arches and settle my weight.

But I looked even more like a fairy.

Matthilda sighed. "Too bad. He would look so lovely with a dress and make up."

"I know," Lannie agreed. "But he just isn't that kind of man."

"They all are if you withhold sex long enough."

"Do you think I should try?"

There was a silence while they all contemplated that, and I started to shiver. I didn't like the way this thing was going.

I finished the living room, and it was four in the morning. Most of the ladies had gone home. They had put their clothes in the wash, and as the clothes came out they put them on and went home. Except for Matthilda. Matthilda had her clothes, but for some reason she was spending the night in the guest room. that left me, and Lannie, and I was exhausted. But how was I going to sleep with this thing in my butt?

Nobody cared.

"Good night, Ron." Lannie headed for the bedroom. I heard the door close, and the lock click.

I stood there, then went to the couch. It smelled of cleaner, but I managed to get down, turn on my side on the thing. I was still arched, my butt pulled up, but I could sleep. If I could forget about this thing massaging my insides, and the fact that my dick was standing up and crowing like a rooster.

The next morning, I had to fix breakfast for Matthilda and Lannie. I was not allowed in the kitchen after I had served them, and I heard the murmur of their voices as they talked. I heard my name a couple of times, and it was obvious they were talking about me. But what were they saying? I found out soon enough.

"Let's go, Ronald." Matthilda strode out of the kitchen.

"What? Where?"

"You have to clean houses. You defiled a lot of women, and you have to make up for it. So get your ass in gear and let's go."

I followed her out the front door. Her car was in the driveway, and we had tall shrubs, but I was still...naked and afraid.

Still, I had no choice. I walked down the cement walk to her car.

She ignored me and was talking to Lannie.

I opened the front door...

"What do you think you're doing?"

"Getting in the car." I sounded so hopeless and befuddled.

"Back seat."

"Oh." I closed the front, opened the back, and crawled in. I couldn't sit down, all I could do was kneel on all fours. My head was down, my back was arched, and I just knelt there.

A few minutes later Matthilda got in, said good bye to Lannie, and we were off.

"Let's see," she mused. "Should I go to the farm and let you clean that? Or just stay in town? Hmmm. Let me think."

While she thought she drove around corners, and I swayed and nearly lost my balance. Then she stopped suddenly, and I was pushed against the back of the front seats.

And she hit potholes and speed bumps and I was jounced and bounced and my poor ass didn't feel so sexy.

Finally, she drove up a driveway, and into a garage. She got out and opened my door. "Let's go." And I had a big problem.

I had crawled into the car from the passenger side. To get out I needed to back out the passenger side. But the passenger side was up against a wall, no way to open that door. I was going to have to get out on the driver's side, but if I did that I was going to have to go out head first!

For long minutes I struggled, tried to get out, and, finally, I managed to turn around. I backed out, then walked, on my high heels towards the door leading into the house.

"Well, it's about time," Matthilda was sitting at the kitchen table, reading a book. "Follow me."

I followed her, my heels tapping on the kitchen floor, into the living room.

She had a big, ranch style home, and she dropped articles of clothing on the floor and headed for a couch. Now naked, she turned and sat down and spread her legs.

"Might just as well clean this, first."

"What? But…"

"What? You don't like pussy? Lannie said you were carrying on and acting the fool over not getting a little pussy. Here I am, offering you a lot, and you act like a fool! Now get down and clean me out!"

I used the edge of the couch to get down, then I knee walked around and between her legs.

She sighed and laid back, and I moved in.

I like eating pussy. I loved the fresh smell of pussy sweat. I love the delicate skin and the way it responds to my tongue. I love the way women—Lannie—arches her back and cums all over my face.

But this was old pussy. It didn't smell sweet and fresh, like perfume. It smelled old, like a worn shoe. And the skin was not as soft; it was tough. And the aroma coming out was like a barn that needed to be mucked, and the juices that bubbled…they were like kitchen grease.

"I usually don't smell like this," smiled Matthilda. "I didn't wash yesterday, however, for I knew you'd appreciate an earthy, old lady smell."

I touched my lips to her labia and almost puked.

"Ahh. Yes. I haven't had a good eat job in a while. She grabbed my head and pulled me tighter into her.

I gagged, and gobbled. I licked things that had the texture of slugs. I sucked on her clit, which was over-sized with age and like sucking on a pointy thimble.

"Oh, yeah. She was right. You do have some use. Now use that tongue!"

I licked, I lapped. I poked and prodded. I sampled and tasted, and managed not to disgorge my innards into her love canal. Hell, she'd just make me lap it up if I did.

"Yeah, baby. Do it!"

She was getting carried away, pulling my hair, hard, and forcing my face into her pussy again and again. Her hips started to writhe and pump.

"Yeah! Fuck me with your nose!"

She maneuvered my head so my nose was actually going into her cunt. I couldn't breath, and I gasped for air with my mouth. My mouth, of course, was right over her asshole.

Oh, God! I thought. *Please don't fart!*

Trying to hold my breath, gasping for air periodically, her pussy ground into my face. Finally, she started to spasm. The muscles in her thighs tightened and her thighs clamped over my face.

She came, a gusher, and she pounded on my head and kept smashing her pussy into my face.

And...right when she was all done, starting to relax...she farted.

Of course.

I gagged and felt convulsions twisting my belly.

She pushed me away and gave a groan of satisfaction. "Nice. We'll have to do this again."

She opened her eyes and grinned at me. "You wouldn't mind being the official pussy cleaner for The Ladies' Sissy Society?"

I just knelt on the rug, on all fours like a dog, my butt pulled up and my head raised to relieve some of the tension on the cord to the butt hook.

"I...I..."

"Don't bother answering. We'll probably make that decision for you. Men shouldn't be trusted to make important decisions. Right?"

"Uh..."

She laughed. "Don't worry. You'll get used to it, and you'll wonder how you ever existed before we got our mitts on you. Now, the cleaning tools for my house are in closet in the kitchen hallway. I want the bathroom spic and span. The kitchen, of course, should receive loving care. I'm going to want vacuuming and dusting, the furniture polished, and, oh, yes, the pool needs cleaning.

And there I was, my face smelling like 60 year old pussy. My dick dripping like a broken faucet, unable to do anything but kneel on all fours.

And I was a maid. Of sorts. And I had a feeling that, once the butt hook was out I would probably be in a maid's uniform. I just sort of surmised that.

These women, you see, weren't about to back off.

The Ladies Sissy Society was the real deal, and they were no nonsense bitches who knew how to make a man jump to their tune.

So I cleaned Matthilda's house. Then Sandra came and collected me. I spent a day cleaning her house, and she walked around naked and laughed at my drooling penis. And then there was Jocelyn and Jane, and Tandy and Morgan and...and I cleaned the houses, and the pussies, of all those women.

Then I was returned to my wife.

I crept in the front door on all fours, head down and butt up.

"Well, look what the cat dragged in."

I crept past my laughing wife, down the hallway, and into the bedroom. I managed to crawl up on the bed and lay on my side, stretched out and penetrated and totally discouraged.

I closed my eyes, and wished for this terrible time to end. I had had enough of walking around with a butt hook up my ass. I had sucked enough pussy for a lifetime. I had cleaned too many houses and wanted no more.

And I wanted relief. My poor cock and balls were inflamed, eternally excited, and I just wanted…I just wanted…I drifted away.

"Honey?" The bed was shaking gently. "Honey?"

Wait, I wasn't in bed. I was…somewhere else! Where was I?

"Open your eyes, baby. I want to talk to you."

I jerked and came awake. I was in the easy chair in the basement. I was in the muumuu, and several empty bottles of Golden Monkey were on the floor next to me.

"What?" Dazed, I sat up, and the hook wasn't in my butt anymore!

"I talked to Matthilda, and she said you're the kind of guy that needs sex. You're not a sissy, and…well, you have needs."

"I…what? She said that?"

I was wearing the muumuu, and my cock was hard. There was no sign of the chains on the wall. And my butt…my butt! It was free!

"She did. So do you want to come up and…maybe we could…you know?"

I sat up straight, my eyes wide, I wasn't hooked! I hadn't cleaned houses! I hadn't been forced to eat pussy!

"Ron? Are you all right?"

"Yeah…yeah…" I looked around in amazement. It had all been a dream! A Golden Monkey induced dream! I had dreamed of throwing up on The Ladies Sissy Society! And pissing on them! And I hadn't just spent a week cleaning their houses and…and eating them out!

"Would you like to go upstairs?"

I looked around, amazed, dazed, stunned.

I had dreamed it all!

"Do you?"

I looked at my lovely wife. I stared at the basement. A dream.

"Uh…could I drink a Golden Monkey, first?"

END

A Note from the Author!

I hope you liked these little gems.
Please take a moment to rate me five stars.
That helps support my writing,
and lets me know which direction I should take
for future books.

Thank you

Grace

Story too short?
Didn't want it to end?
Then check out these

FULL LENGTH NOVELS!

on the following pages.
And if you want to stick with the shorts,
scroll past the novels
and you will find BIG collections
of the finest erotica in the world!
SCROLL DOWN

FULL LENGTH BOOKS!

THE classic of feminization.

Alex is ensnared by an internet stalker. Day after day he is forced to feminize. His neighbor finds out and the situation becomes worse. Now his wife is due home, and he doesn't know what to do. What's worse, he is starting to like it.

Sissy Ride: The Book!

Roscoe was a power player in Hollywood. He was handsome, adored, and had one fault - he liked to play practical jokes. Now his wife is playing one on him, and it's going to be the grandest practical joke of all time.
I Changed My Husband into a Woman

Kindle customers said: Told first-person by loving but vengeful wife of rich cheating husband…Excellent read for forced-fem lovers…the deflowering was perfect.

FULL LENGTH BOOKS!

Randy catches his wife cheating, but a mysterious woman is about to take him in hand and teach him that when a woman cheats…it is the man's fault.

The Big Tease!

Sam thought he was a tough guy. He was cock of the walk, a real, live, do or die Mr. Tough Guy.

Then he made a mistake. He took on the wrong … woman.

This is the story of what happened when Sam finally met his match and learned who the really tough people are.

Too Tough to Feminize

Carol said: Ms Mansfield certainly understands the full force of female superiority and empowerment !

I felt myself surrendering to the 'woman in me', and wanting to be a part of a dynamic woman's world.

FULL LENGTH BOOKS!

Jim Camden was a manly man, until the day he crossed his wife. Now he's in for a battle of the sexes, and if he loses…he has to dress like a woman for a week. But what he doesn't know is the depths of manipulation his wife will go to. Lois Camden, you see, is a woman about to break free, and if she has to step on her husband to do it…so be it. And Jim is about to learn that a woman unleashed is a man consumed.

The Feminization Games

Tom Dickson was a happy camper. He lived a good life, had a beautiful wife, then he started to grow breasts, his hair grew long, and his body reshaped. Now Tom is on the way to being a woman, and he doesn't know why.

My Husband's Funny Breasts

MY HUSBAND'S FUNNY BREASTS

It's not so funny when
it's happening to you!

GRACE MANSFIELD

FULL LENGTH BOOKS!

Rick Boston and his beautiful wife, Jamey, move to Stepforth Valley, where Rick is offered a job at a high tech cosmetics company. The House of Chimera is planning on releasing a male cosmetics line, and Rick is their first test subject. Now Rick is changing. The House of Chimera has a deep, dark secret, and Rick is just one more step on the path to world domination!

The Stepforth Husband

Grace Mansfield

The Stepforth Husband

Robert said: I was expecting less and got more! Having knowledge of the original story I made some assumptions. Intricate emotions and some a few twists later and Ms Mansfield has a good book on her hands.

Alex has to live in an old, decrepit mansion for the summer. Worse, he's supposed to follow the directions of an old biddy who, right off the bat, makes him wear girl clothes!

Alex is in for a surprise, however, because the house is haunted, and wearing girl clothes is the least of what is going to happen to him!

Feminized by a Ghost

Feminized by a Ghost

Grace Mansfield

FULL LENGTH BOOKS!

This is the second book in the Stepforth Series. The first book is 'The Stepforth Husband.'

Judd is the product of the Amazons. the Amazons are an ancient race of women who are working for the betterment of mankind.

Judd must go to Stepforth Valley and uncover an insidious plot to make the men of the world into women. He will be chemically changed, betrayed by those who love him, and, in the end, come to the truth of the world.

Revenge of the Stepforth Husbands

A Kindle Customer said of The Stepforth Husband and the Revenge of the Stepforth Husbands: This two book set is an intriguing blending of erotica, adventure, mystery and philosophy. Sated you will be regarding the first three categories and if your world or life views can accept it, be intrigued by the author's theological speculations as described at the end of the second book. Fiction is always made more interesting when it is based in truth.

There are MORE full length novels at:

GROPPER PRESS

BUT…
if you want save money
check out the following link…

Big Erotic Collections!

You'll find massive collections
of the finest erotica in the world!
Just like the ones on the following pages.

BIG COLLECTIONS!

Save money
SEVEN sexy stories
A sorority that feminizes...'Tootsie' goes all the way...National lipstick day and all the men in Hollywood start growing breasts...learning to be a man by being a woman, and more, more, more.

The Electric Groin!

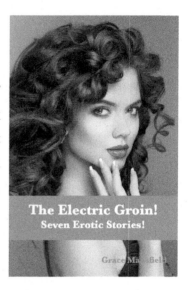

The Electric Groin!
Seven Erotic Stories!

Save money with SEVEN erotic stories
Men turning into women because of the vaccine...a woman makes her husband wear a chastity device, then they swap bodies...feminization training... feminized by his sister...and more, more!

Quivering Buns

Quivering Buns
Seven Erotic Stories!

BIG COLLECTIONS!

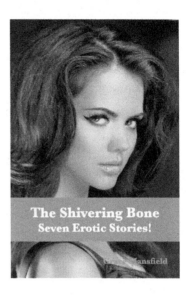
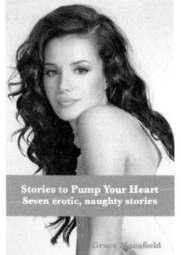

BIG COLLECTIONS!

The Best Erotica in the World is at...
GROPPER PRESS

Following is a list of stories from Gropper Press.
Many of them are five star,
all of them are hot and steamy!

https://gropperpress.wordpress.com

Big Stories

<u>The Day the Democrats Turned the Republicans into...Girls!</u> ~ A note from Grace...I got tired of all the politics on TV, everybody yelling at everybody, and everybody knowing they are the only ones that are right...it's enough to make a girl pick up an erotic book. You know? So, are you ready for the 'transgenderment' of half the country?

Long Island Reader said: Certainly different! This book was unlike any gender swap story I have read before. It is well written and quite sexy, but more than that, it is suffused with a sense of humor that really captures our current political dichotomy. What a concept! Be you a Democrat or a Republican, I suggest reading this with an open mind. Wow!

Big Stories

Feminized for Granny ~ Underwear is disappearing from Joanna's department store. She catches the culprit, and a spanking reveals that Eric is a cross dresser. Joann realizes there is something very hot about cross dressing, but how far can she push Eric?

Je said: Well written, the story flowed well with believable text. I enjoyed the concept of the story and the emotional turmoil of the the people.

Feminized for Granny!
Revenge, lust and...Grandma?

Grace Mansfield

Feminized in 100 Days ~ Tom loves his wife, but he doesn't feel worthy. She is so beautiful and powerful. Tammi learns how Tom feels, and comes up with a plan to make Tom feel beautiful and worthy, and It only takes 100 days.

A wonderful tale of erotic sex and the exchange of power.

A kindle customer said: Every man should have a wonderful wife to walk through life by "her" side! I didn't want the story to end!

Feminized in 100 Days
Love and the Exchange of Power

Mansfield

Big Stories

Feminized Cop ~ SAM wasn't big enough to be a real cop, so he became T-Rex, a feminized cop. Drugs, guns and sex…he's in the middle of it. But when he tries to get out, that's when the trouble starts, and that's when he finds out what being a feminized cop really means.

This is a steamy, rock and roll story about a straight man learning to walk on the wild side!

Feminized Cop!
It was a job a man couldn't do

The Were-Fem ~ RODNEY paid no attention when his parents said 'Don't go in the woods. He enters the woods and is captivated by a naked girl swimming in a pond. She takes him to a mysterious castle and he is…changed. By day he is a hard working lad, but at night he becomes something else!

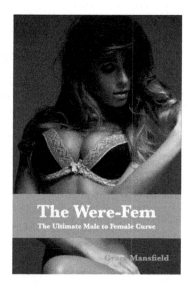

The Were-Fem
The Ultimate Male to Female Curse

Big Stories

I Changed My Nephew into a Woman!
~ MARTHA gets a call from her sister, and is asked to look out for her nephew for a summer. She is not happy, but she talks to her friend, Daphne, and they start making plans. Then the nephew shows up, and they get the surprise of their lives. Chuckie wants something that only they can provide, and he is willing to do what they want to get it!

I Changed My Nephew into a Woman!

Johnny Gets Taken Down
~ JOHNNY loves his wife, and he loves to cross dress. But when a Mystery Hacker takes over his computer and finds his hidden stash of selfies, his world comes undone. Johnny is forced to wear dresses, to wear a chastity tube, and even to make love to his Ex. But when the end comes it is something that Johnny never expected. The identity of the Mystery Hacker turns out to be the biggest shocker of all!

Johnny Gets Taken Down!
A forced feminization ending you will never forget!

If you liked

'The Pink Path!'

you will really love...

'I Changed My Husband into a Woman'

A full length novel by Grace Mansfield

Here is an excerpt...

"What the fuck!"

I roused myself from a deep and very deserved sleep, only to see Roscoe standing next to the bed, looking down at his feet and cursing.

"Wha..." I mumbled, pulling the covers over me and trying to look like I was still asleep. In truth, though I was tired, I was as awake as I had ever been.

"Did you do this?" His voice was going up. "Is this your idea of a joke?"

"Shut up," I whined. "I wanna sleep!"

"No! Wake up! Why'd you do this?"

"Do what?" and I finally rolled over and made my eyes sleepy and tired.

Oh, baby, was I acting. And I was acting in front of the fellow who had created a half a dozen Best Actor Oscar winners. This was going to take all my prowess to pull off.

"My toes! Look at my toes."

I blinked, and edged towards the side of the bed so I could look down to where he was pointing. And I exulted. He had felt he had to explain that it was his toes, so he was just working off emotion and blaming whoever was closest. He didn't have any clue as to why his toes were red.

"What the fuck!" I opened my eyes wide and stared at his tootsies.

"Why'd you do this?"

I looked up at him and put a tiny edge of anger in my voice. "I didn't do that! Why the hell would I paint my sissy husband's toes red?" Very important to get the word sissy into the conversation as quickly as possible. "Do I look like I'm the kind of girl who'd marry a sissy?"

He kept trying to look fierce, but I could tell that my arrows had hit the mark. In some odd, almost invisible way he shriveled. He withdrew slightly into himself. I had met the challenge and acted my way out of being the culprit.

"Okay, okay," then he tried again. "You did this because I jacked off on you the other day."

"First, I just said I didn't do that!" I pointed at his toes. "And, I already got you back, and, husband of mine, practical jokes aren't my forte." At least they usually weren't. I was enjoying this; I was thinking of a career change. Sandy Tannenbaum, Practical Joker Extraordinaire!

"So who did this?"

Now I looked at him suspiciously. "There's only two people in this room."

He sputtered in outrage, so I kept up the attack. "So why did you paint your toe nails red?"

"I didn't!"

"There's nobody else here!" I was pushing him now. I had been accused unfairly (he thought) so I had to act the outrage. I narrowed my eyes. "Are you going pervert on me?"

"I didn't do this!" he wailed.

"Well I didn't, and I didn't figure on waking up next to Bruce Jenner."

Oh, Jesus!" he almost ran to my make up station and started looking for polish remover. "Where is it!?"

I got out of bed, and went to him. I didn't want him making a mess, so I handed him a bottle of polish remover. He grabbed at it like a sailor grabs a life preserver after jumping off the Titanic. He sat down and lifted his foot up to the edge of the chair.

"Hold on," I said. I took the remover out of his hands. "I don't want you making a mess. Come here."

I led him into the bathroom. "Put your foot here," I pointed to the john. He placed his foot on the toilet and I sat cross legged in front of it. I giggled.

"What?" he groused.

"It is sort of cute. Hubbie gives himself a peddie. Make a good TV series."

He let his breath out in disgust. "I'm a man's man, not a girly man."

Yeah, that's right, you like to get young girl's pregnant. how manly. But I didn't say that, I just thought it, and kept manipulating him.

"Well, you might say so, but Roscoe Junior says otherwise."

Now, truth, he wasn't really all that hard, just sort of a morning half woodie, but I reached up and grabbed his meat and in a second he was throbbing in my hand.

"Hey!" he said. But he wasn't really protesting. What man would object to a pair of sexy hands fondling his man pole? "Take the polish off."

"Oh, okay." but the damage was done. He was now erect, and associating that erection with nail polish. Manly man. Huh!

So I hummed a tune and stripped the polish off and returned his toes to their 'manly' state.

"Okay," he said. Standing and looking down at his repaired manhood, uh, nails.

"Not even a thanks?"

"Thank you," and he did sound abashed. "But I have no idea how… somebody must have broken in and done it."

"While you slept? They painted your nails and you didn't even wake up?"

"Well, I was pretty drunk."

I'll say.

"Not that drunk," I lied. "You never get that drunk."

"Well, yeah. But somebody did it." We left the bathroom then and re-entered the bedroom. He walked over to the double windows, which led out to a small patio. He tried the doors. "See! they're open!"

"We're on the second floor."

"He had a ladder."

"He?"

"Well, you don't think a woman did this?"

"Those nails were done pretty well. Men don't know how to apply polish that well." Then I cocked my head and it was obvious what I was thinking.

"Don't look at me that way! I didn't polish my own nails."

I shrugged. "Okay. So Spiderman left off fighting crime for one day so he could paint your nails."

He made a grimace.

"Or maybe somebody just walked in because our door is unlocked." I swung the bedroom door opened.

"Well, I don't…"

"Forget it, Roscoe." I use his name when I am angry with him, or irritated, and he took notice of that. "just admit that you did some sleep walking." Then I giggled, "Or sleep toenail painting."

"Oh, shut up." he brushed past me and headed down the stairs. It was a mark of how irritated and upset he was that he had forgotten to get dressed.

"Ahem!" I cleared my throat.

He turned at the top of the stairs and looked at me. Oh, the look on his face. Irritated, confused. Priceless.

I looked at his groin, placed an elbow in a palm and wiggled my index finger in the air.

He looked down at himself, mumbled a curse word I dasn't dare repeat, and stomped back into the bedroom.

This has been an excerpt from

I Changed My Husband into a Woman!

Read it on kindle or paperback

Made in the USA
Las Vegas, NV
26 March 2022

46357744R00095